# Nowhere for Christmas

## by

## Heather Gray

Nowhere for Christmas
by Heather Gray
Published by Astraea Press
www.astraeapress.com

*in celebration of my Savior*
*in memory of my daughter*
*with pride in my son*
*with gratitude for my husband*

*When Pharaoh finally let the people go, God did not lead them along the main road that runs through Philistine territory, even though that was the shortest route to the Promised Land. God said, "If the people are faced with a battle, they might change their minds and return to Egypt." So God led them in a roundabout way through the wilderness toward the Red Sea.*

~Exodus 13: 17-18a

# Chapter One

Albuquerque, NM
December 22

*Some women are satisfied with one man in their life. There are even women who would say that's too many. Not me, though. Oh, no. Not me. I get to juggle two.*

Avery Weston stormed into her editor's office and slammed the door behind her. Mitchell peered up from his catastrophe of a desk. The newsroom had been battling mice off and on for two years now, but Mitchell's office remained rodent-free. Her theory? *The little beasts are terrified of getting squashed under a falling stack of paper, or worse, getting lost in this mess and starving to death.*

Mitchell, bushy black eyebrows raised, inspected her and asked, "Yes, Avery?"

She threw herself into the only chair not filled with file folders, books, and other paraphernalia. "I got your memo. You didn't have the guts to tell me in person?"

His eyes returned to the article he was reviewing, red pen in hand. Mitchell was old enough to be her... big brother...

but he insisted on doing things *old school*. There was no way he'd ever get caught editing important articles on his computer. He wanted a printout in one hand and his red pen in the other. "I thought your temper might cool down during the walk from your desk to my office."

"You thought wrong."

"I see that." Mitchell laid his red pen down on top of the printout he'd been studying. "Has it occurred to you this might be fun?"

"Has it occurred to you I might look for a job elsewhere?" She'd worked for Mitchell more years than she could remember. He'd given her the start she'd desperately needed, and because of him, she was able to provide for the other man in her life. They both knew she wouldn't be looking for a job elsewhere, but that didn't stop her from voicing the empty threat now and then.

"Think of it as an adventure."

*Yeah, right.* "Have you spent much time with teenagers recently?"

Mitchell removed his glasses and pinched the bridge of his nose. "Is that the problem? You don't think Eli will want to go?"

Avery sighed and sank back into the chair she occupied. "He's fifteen, Mitchell. I told him we'd go north for Christmas so he could go skiing. Now I'm going to be hauling him across three states to a Podunk town in the middle of nowhere. Nowhere! Do you have any idea exactly how *not* happy he is going to be with me?"

Mitchell opened his mouth to say something.

Avery, ignoring him, continued her monologue. "He's not going to blame you, either. Eli won't think *Mom has such a rotten boss. How dare he ruin my Christmas plans?*" She let out a sigh and said, "This is all going to be my fault as far as he's concerned. I will have broken my word to him, and he will have one more reason to resent me for the rest of his life."

This time Mitchell lifted a hand to stop Avery so he could say something.

Again dismissing his action, she said, "Do you have any idea how hard it is to raise a teenage boy alone? Or to raise any child alone for that matter? He wasn't always a teenager, you know. Eli started out as a baby, and I thought how hard it was to be a single mom to this tiny little thing that cried and pooped all the time. I never slept. No matter how hard it got, I provided a home for him because he was my responsibility, my joy. Then he was in grade school, and I thought that was as hard as it could possibly get. I worked ten hours a day for a tyrant of a boss, then came home to fix dinner for my finicky son and spend three hours working on homework with him so he could pass to the next grade."

Mitchell cleared his throat.

Avery kept talking. "You know, when I was in school, we didn't start working on algebra until I was in junior high. Eli started working basic algebra equations in second grade. Who does that? Algebra in second grade! Sure, it was easy stuff, but whatever happened to being a child? But I did it. I wanted the best for my son. I looked at it as an exercise in building confidence as he put in the hard work and saw it pay off, so I sat there with him for hours and hours every night. Because I'm his mom. Has he ever noticed any of that? Of course not! He notices everything he *doesn't* get in this life. And now, thanks to you, he gets to add skiing trip to the list of things to hold against me. You're a peach, Mitchell! An absolute peach."

As her voice wound down, Avery eyed Mitchell and saw he had gone back to editing the article he'd been looking at when she'd come in.

"Are you listening to anything I say?" When Mitchell said nothing, she leaned forward and slapped her palm against the edge of his desktop. She didn't use much force, but the impact still vibrated up her arm and echoed among the stacks of files and papers around the room.

Her editor neither jumped nor reacted. Instead, the picture of calm, he put his pen down, took his glasses off, and set them next to the pen. Taking his time, he looked up and asked, "Are you done yet?"

She tried to stare him down, but he was having none of it.

Mitchell leaned back in his chair and crossed his arms over his chest. "I'm not an entirely insensitive clod, despite what you may think. Sending you off to chase a story over Christmas isn't my idea. This came down from higher up, and I don't have a say in it. Apparently the Quaint American Towns feature you've been doing for the past year has gotten a good-enough response that the big wigs at Corporate are following through on their promise of syndication and have given me a list of towns and times they want you to cover in the coming year. They're insisting the national syndication of your feature start with this particular story, and they demand it be authentically at Christmas. I did my best to cull down the list and eliminate some of the ones that would take you out of town for extended trips during the school year. Corporate would not, however, budge on the Christmas trip. In fact, they went so far as to make it a contingency of your national syndication."

When Avery started to sputter again, Mitchell held up his hand to silence her. "Contrary to popular opinion, I do have sympathy. You drive down tomorrow, spend Christmas eve and day, drive back the day after, and then you'll have the rest of his break to take the kid skiing. Besides, I already called Eli and told him about the trip. I wanted to make sure he understood it was coming from me, that you didn't have a choice in the matter."

"You spoke to my son about this?" Avery's voice was filled with skepticism.

A bark of laughter escaped as Mitchell shook his head and answered, "Two days ago. I guess he didn't mention it to you?"

"My son has known my job assignment for two days, and I am just now finding out about it?"

Mitchell shrugged. "Hey, I told him to pass the information on to you. The memo was nothing more than the official documentation so Corporate has the nice paper trail they prefer."

Avery ran a hand through her light brown hair, not at all embarrassed by her previous rant. "I suppose it's a good thing we're friends, and you can't fire me, huh? If any other reporter came in here and went off on you like that, they'd be out of here in a heartbeat, wouldn't they?"

Raising an eyebrow, Mitchell replied, "I guess we can all be thankful you closed the door when you came in."

Something in his voice warned Avery she wasn't going to be happy with what she would see. She spun around to look at the door. There it was, standing wide open. Turning to look at her boss, she said, "I did it again, didn't I?"

He nodded.

Swallowing, she leaned back in her chair. "I'm not a very good example to your other employees." This wasn't the first time Avery had slammed the door so hard it had bounced back open rather than shut.

"Which is why I always tell them to do the exact opposite of whatever you do. Unless they're on assignment. Then they can emulate you," he said with a wink.

"I can't believe Eli has known for two days and said nothing to me." Her voice was rueful, all trace of her previous drama gone.

"You know he's somewhere howling in laughter over this. He probably has the office bugged, and we don't even know it."

Avery shook her head. "Even the bugs are afraid of your office," she said, her voice dry. "I don't think he could have convinced any to stay in here." She adjusted her scarf and asked, "Has Gavin been yet to take the pictures? It helps if I can see the photos first so I know which parts of the town to include in my piece."

Mitchell's pronounced eyebrows climbed up again. "You didn't read the entire memo, did you?" She shook her head, and he said, "Gavin's traveling with you. This was a last-minute push by Corporate, and he hasn't had a chance to get out there ahead of you, so he's going to have to go with you."

Avery had a sinking feeling and could have sworn she felt a large stone being dropped into her stomach with a loud *kplunk*.

Gavin Eastly had once been a rising star in photojournalism. He'd fallen off the radar a couple years back and had only recently started working again. The fact that he was doing work for the Albuquerque Times spoke to how far from grace he'd fallen. She didn't know the story behind it, but when someone as good at their job as he'd been disappears as suddenly as he had, the assumption tended to be a stint in rehab or a mental hospital. Maybe both.

She bit her lip before saying, "Mitchell, I've never met Gavin. The only things I know about him are the photos he takes… and his reputation. I'm not sure I want to be confined with him for such a long trip." Her editor watched her but didn't say anything. *I hate it when he does that. It always makes me say more than I intend.* "My teenage son will be with me. What if Gavin has… bad habits… that might influence my son?"

His lips twitched, and she had the feeling he was trying not to laugh at her.

"Gavin's story is his own to tell," he said.

This time it was her turn to cross her arms and stare.

With a camaraderie built from years working together, Mitchell sat back, his muscles loose and relaxed, as he looked her in the eye and said, "You don't have to worry about Gavin being a bad influence on Eli."

"I need something more than that. You ought to know

that about me."

Mitchell ran a hand through his thinning hair and said, "Close the door."

Surprised by the command, Avery rose to shut the door then pulled her chair closer to the desk so she didn't miss anything Mitchell had to say.

"Gavin is family."

Avery's stomach fluttered akin to when she was on the scent of a big story. "Family?"

"On my wife's side. That's all I can tell you, and you need to keep it quiet."

"Why is it a secret?"

"It's complicated."

"Smoking, drinking, drugs? Anything I should watch for?"

"I wouldn't be sending you anywhere with him if he had any dangerous issues. He's clean, Avery. And a good guy. He's having a hard time right now is all."

"Mental breakdown? Do I need to make sure the knives are removed from the table whenever we stop to eat?"

His eyes narrowed and he said, voice deeper than usual, "He's an amazing photographer, good enough to make even the ugliest town look beautiful." The easy posture was gone as Mitchell leaned forward and said, "Don't give him any grief, and do your best not to ask questions. That's all I'm willing to say about it."

*I'm not going to let it drop that easily, and you know it.*

"Fine. I'll go. When do we leave, and whose car are we taking?"

Mitchell sat back, his brow wrinkling. "Uh, I've lined up a rental. It's in your name, and they will come pick you up at your house tomorrow morning at ten. Gavin is supposed to text you in the A.M. to let you know where to pick him up."

"Sounds like a plan," she said with a smile. "Thanks for setting everything up!"

Avery breezed out of Mitchell's office with a triumphant smile on her face. She'd left him guessing, and she knew it. He couldn't hide his surprise or suspicion, and that suited her fine. *I'll drop my questions about Gavin when purple monkeys start dancing on the hood of my rental car.*

# Chapter Two

"Eli!" she called when she got home. No answer. "Eli! Where are you?" Still no answer.

*It's not as if the house is so big he's too far away to hear!*

She stepped into her son's room and saw him sitting on his bed, back leaning against the wall, earbuds firmly in place. *Someday we're going to have to get those things surgically removed.* Avery wrapped her knuckles against his door, and Eli lifted his eyes.

When he saw her, he had the decency to remove one of his earbuds and ask, "What's up, Mom?"

"You need to pack. We're leaving on a trip tomorrow."

Eli jerked his head, pointing it toward the wall behind her. Avery turned to see his suitcase. "You're already packed?"

"Uh, duh. Isn't that obvious?"

She rolled her eyes.

"Careful," he said. "They might get stuck in the back of your head."

She gave him *The Look.*

Instead of squirming the way he would when he was

9

eight years old, he laughed. "Come on, Mom. I'm telling you what you always tell me. If you roll your eyes too much, they'll get stuck in the back of your head, and you'll never be able to see anything but your brain ever again."

*I did this to myself. I tried to raise the boy with humor. That was before I realized he'd eventually get old enough to start turning it back on me. What was I thinking?*

"Did you pack a toothbrush?"

He shrugged. "I put a new one in so I wouldn't have to worry about it."

"You sure you've got everything? Should we go through it?"

"Yes, I packed enough underwear, but if you want to count, go ahead. Just be sure to put everything back the way you found it when you're done. I don't want to have to repack afterward."

She backed out of his room to go take care of her own packing, then stopped and popped back over the threshold. "I gave Mitchell a huge lecture today about how he was ruining your Christmas. He let me go on and on about it. The whole my-son-will-hate-me-forever speech." Eli's lips twitched. "Were you ever going to tell me you'd spoken to him?"

"Nah. I know how much you enjoy ranting. Figured I was doing you a favor by giving you a reason."

"Did he at least tell you the name of the town we're heading to?" When Eli shook his head, Avery took great delight in saying, "We're heading to Nowhere, Oklahoma."

If she wasn't mistaken, her son paled a bit at her words. "Who names a town Nowhere?"

She shrugged and said, "We'll find out when we get there."

"Will they even have electricity? Will I be able to charge my phone and MP3 player?" Eli squinted his eyes at her before saying, "Nah. You're pulling my leg. That can't be for real."

Avery shook her head and laughed as she headed down

the hall. "Give me twenty minutes to pack, then I'll fix dinner!" she called back over her shoulder. When she got no response, she figured the earbuds had been safely replaced. Either that, or Eli was trying to come up with an excuse to get out of eating. *If I'd had his aversion to well-balanced meals as a child,, I'd have starved to death!*

****

Thirty minutes later, Avery conceded defeat. She'd noticed but hadn't really registered the size of Eli's suitcase. Then she'd gone to pack her own bag. By the time she'd added her laptop, tablet, notebook for jotting down ideas, and a couple reading books into it, Avery had no room left for her clothes. As she studied the faded green cloth of the suitcase nestled among the piles of clothes on her bed, she realized something. "Eli!"

"What's up, Mom?"

"You took my suitcase!"

"I needed room for all my stuff."

"I'm standing here trying to figure out why everything won't fit, and it's because you left me with the small suitcase."

"Come on, Mom. You had to realize what size it was when you picked it up and put it on your bed. And you even saw the other suitcase in my room. It's not like I was hiding it or anything."

Avery stared at him, blinking. He was spot-on, but there was no way she was going to tell him so.

"I'm going to have to go get the other big one out of the attic," she said with a sigh, hoping her son would volunteer to climb up in there and retrieve it for her.

Instead, he nodded and asked, "You want me to pull the ladder down for you?" She grinned to herself as she nodded. They had a regular battle about the attic. Neither of them liked going up there. Since he'd gone up to retrieve all the

Christmas decorations earlier in the month, she'd let him have the victory this time.

After Avery scaled the creaky ladder up into the attic, she scanned the web-dusted contents, quickly locating the suitcase she needed. It was older and more faded than the green one, and it had a rust-and-mustard-colored seventies floral pattern on it. *At least no one will try to steal it.*

As she dragged the suitcase with its one broken wheel across the attic floor, a cloud of who-knew-what gently puffed up into the air around her. Then she got a mouthful of it and started coughing, which led to more grime and dust billowing into the air. That, of course, led to more coughing.

Avery lost her balance and started to fall out of the attic opening, but the suitcase blocked her way enough to pause her descent, giving her time to reach out and grab the back of an old chair that had been in the attic longer than they'd lived in the house. The suitcase wasn't so lucky. It fell zipper-over-wheel down the attic ladder and landed with a loud *thud* on the carpeted floor below.

By the time Avery pulled herself back to her feet and made her way down the ladder, she expected to find Eli standing there wondering where his dinner was. Alas, her teen was blissfully unaware of her near-death-by-attic experience. He was in his room listening to his MP3 player. *It's for the best. I wouldn't want him to pull a muscle laughing at me.*

****

Eli and Avery sat down at the dinner table. Regardless of how busy their lives got, she insisted they eat at the table whenever they were both home together. No television, radio, MP3 player, or computer. Just the two of them.

On cue, Eli said, "Come on, Mom. It's only music. What's wrong with listening to music while I eat?"

Avery offered a wide smile and said, "Well, *son*, I would

enjoy spending this time visiting with you. That's hard to do when you're listening to someone else instead of me."

He set the MP3 player on the table. She continued to look at it pointedly until he grudgingly reached over to power it down. When the screen was black, she asked, "Would you care to say the blessing?"

"Sure," he answered. Then, bowing his head, he said, "Dear God, please bless this food to our bodies. Bless the hands that prepared it. Help Mom's cooking not to kill us. Amen."

Avery took a bite of her chicken salad sandwich and said, "One of these days you're going to have to start getting more original when you pray. You've been praying the same prayer since you were ten years old."

"That's not true. Sometimes I ask God to kill my taste buds so I don't hurt your feelings when I taste something new you've cooked." *That's true. He's always been such a thoughtful boy.*

Another bite, and then she said, "So, it'll be you, me, and Gavin. He's the photographer I'll be working with on this one."

Eli's right eyebrow lifted, but all he said was, "I guess that means I'll get the back seat all to myself?"

She shrugged. "Gavin might want the back seat."

"Nah. Adults always want the front, and since you force me to respect my elders, I'll have to let him have it. You ever meet him before?"

"Nope. The car rental place is supposed to come pick us up tomorrow at ten, and Gavin's going to text, letting me know where to collect him."

"What if he turns out to be some creepy old geezer?"

Avery almost spat her baked veggie chip out. When she forced herself to swallow, it went down the wrong pipe. She began coughing until she couldn't breathe. *Great. My cooking might kill one of us yet.*

Tears were rolling down her cheeks by the time she caught her breath and gasped out, "I'm sure he's not a geezer."

Eli laughed. "Great. You're sticking me in a car for hours and hours so I can spend quality time with you and some guy that's probably old and creepy but is not a geezer. This is going to be the best Christmas *ever*."

She'd done a little too good a job raising him to laugh off his troubles. He'd grown into a teen with a cutting wit. As his mom, even she couldn't always tell the difference between when he was joking and being sarcastic. When in doubt, she chose to believe he was suppressing an unquenchable laughter behind words that masqueraded as sardonic.

"Hey, it's four days. You'll still get plenty of time for skiing."

"Are you gonna let me do any of the driving?"

"Uh… will that make a difference in how you treat everyone else in the car?"

"It wasn't going to, but now that you mention it, I think it might. You should let me drive to keep me happy and agreeable."

She polished off the last bite of her sandwich, wiped her hands on her napkin and said, "I'll take that under advisement." *Let the rental agent tell him it's against policy. Then I won't have to be the bad guy.*

"Come on, Mom. This is New Mexico we're talking about. It's not like there's going to be any snow on the ground. Letting me drive would be totally safe. You can think of me as your chauffeur. We'll put the top down, and you can sit back and let the wind flow through your hair while I do all the hard work of driving."

"We are *not* getting a convertible. We're getting a nice sturdy SUV, even if I have to pay the difference out of my own pocket."

"What's wrong with a sports car?"

"A, There's no way on earth I'd ever let you drive it." *So much for letting the rental agency tell him that!* "B, We're going to have three people, their luggage, and no doubt some camera equipment. Unless you plan on riding on the roof, there's no way that's going to happen in a sports car."

Eli picked up his plate and grabbed hers, too, before heading to the kitchen sink. After he put the plates down, he winked at her and said, "I'll be driving. You can ride on the roof. Unless you want to put the creepy old geezer up there. I'm sure we'll be able to find a bungee cord or two to secure him in place. What's the worst that could happen? His denture cream dries up from the wind, and his false teeth get blown out of his mouth? I'm sure even he'd say it's worth it for a sports car."

Avery shook her head as she wiped the table down. "Go grab the green bag out of the front closet and load it up with snacks."

"Isn't the newspaper paying for your meals?"

She gave him a pointed look and said, "I know what a picky eater my son is, and I know things don't always go according to plan. Pack as many snacks in there as you can handle. We'll also take a case of bottled water to be on the safe side."

"My mother," he said as he headed toward the closet, "Over-Planner of the Year."

"Don't knock it, bub. It's kept us out of the poor house and off the evening news, so it must be working."

No different than any other family, they had their moments. For the most part, though, Avery and Eli got along. They joked, had fun, and dissected movies together. After years with just the two of them, they could pretty much complete each other's sentences. Avery knew he was going to grow up and leave home someday. She looked forward to Eli becoming the man God intended him to be, but she knew she'd miss him desperately when the time came. Aside from her job and her faith, he had been her whole life for fifteen years.

When she heard a *thunk* by the front door, Avery poked her head around the corner of the kitchen to see Eli had dropped the green bag there. "Got it all packed with food?"

"Yup."

"Did you pick anything I might be happy to eat, or is it all your favorites?"

He shrugged. "I got a variety. Need me to do anything else?"

"Take out the trash, and then put your suitcase by the front door, too, so we're ready to go in the morning. Since they're not coming till ten, I plan to sleep in."

"You don't sleep in unless you've stayed up till four in the morning reading a book."

"And I've got it already picked out. It's going to be a good one!"

When Eli came back in from emptying the garbage, he noted what Avery was doing and, with an exasperated sigh, raised his eyebrows. "Coffee? You're going to be crabby all day tomorrow if you drink coffee tonight."

"Will not," she replied.

"Uh, yes you will. It's always the same. You drink too much coffee and stay up way too late. Then you get, like, two hours of sleep, and you're in a bad mood the whole next day."

Gazing from Eli to the brewing coffee, she knew he was right. There was no way she was going to admit it, though. She was really looking forward to this book. Even if she wasn't driving the whole trip, she wouldn't get much reading in. Carsickness had plagued her for as long as she could remember. Reading while in a moving vehicle was out of the question. Avery let out a heartfelt sigh and said, "Fine, you win. I'll drink no more than half the pot. I promise."

"Does that mean you'll be in a bad mood for half the day tomorrow or that you'll be in a halfway-bad mood all day?"

She gave him *The Look* again, and he backed out of the kitchen, hands in front of him, "Hey, I'm only asking so I know what to prepare for."

# Chapter Three

December 23, 9:15 a.m.

*Eli will never let me live it down if I tell him he was right. I obviously should have skipped the coffee last night.*

Avery knocked on Eli's bedroom door then opened it. She didn't bother to step into the room when she hollered, "Get-up-or-we're-going-to-be-late." Her words were slurred together from too much fatigue and not enough slumber. Schlepping her way down the hall and into the kitchen, she hoped the haze in her brain would soon clear. To help it along, she promptly started making a pot of coffee. As she inspected the grounds in the filter, she shook her head. *I should have known better.* Then she dumped in two extra scoops of her late-night nemesis and hit the brew button.

She moved back down the hallway and stopped in the bathroom long enough to turn the shower on before going back to her room where she rummaged around for something to wear. Life as a single parent meant all she'd been able to afford was an older house. There was one bathroom, and it took forever for the hot water to reach it. Avery hoped the head start she was giving the pipes would guarantee something hot and steamy upon her return, but she knew better than to expect it. Regardless of temperature, when she got back to the bathroom, she was going to have to climb into the shower if she planned to be ready before the rental car agency came for her and Eli.

When she got into the bathroom, she tested the water. *Still cold.* She hollered down the hallway, "I'm getting in the shower. Make sure you're up by the time I'm out!" If Eli hadn't used the bathroom while she was making the coffee, then he'd simply have to wait until she was out of the shower.

Avery closed the door again and took a quick look in the mirror. *Ugh. When did I get so old?* She had crow's feet inching their way out from the corners of her eyes. *Okay, maybe not inching. That's an exaggeration. They're centimetering their way out. I remember when they were millimetering.* She lathered on her anti-aging face cleaner then stepped into the almost-warm shower. *Maybe we'll stay at a hotel with actual hot water, instead of lukewarm. That would be nice. And complimentary coffee, of course.*

A quick shower, and then Avery was in the kitchen savoring the smell of coffee in her mug as she tried to wait for it to cool down so she could start drinking it. She hollered again, "Eli, are you up yet?" *I love that kid, but it is so stinking hard to get him up in the morning.*

When the sound of movement from Eli's room reached her, followed by the click of the bathroom door, Avery glanced at her watch. Five minutes till ten. She hoped the rental agency was running a couple minutes late.

While Eli was in the shower, she double-checked to make sure the back door was locked, the windows were all closed and latched, and the coffee pot was shut off. She moved her suitcase to the growing pile by the front door.

As if conjured by her thoughts of him, Eli walked into the kitchen looking far too perky for someone who didn't care to get out of bed in the morning. Meanwhile, Avery, normally the morning person, would have rather been anything other than vertical at the moment. Eyeing the clock on the kitchen microwave, she began to wonder where the rental agency people were. It was already twenty after ten. A little bit late was okay. After all, they'd been running pretty late this morning, too. *Don't they usually call if they're behind schedule?*

"Where's the people with the car?" Eli opened the refrigerator while he asked. Without removing anything from the fridge, he closed it and moved to the cupboard where she normally kept oatmeal, sugar, flour, and other baking supplies. *What? Does he think they'd have mixed themselves into muffins while he slept?* After he closed that one, he moved on to the next cupboard. Dried beans, rice, macaroni, and cans of soup.

Avery, who had been trying to hold her laughter in, couldn't fight it anymore. It didn't have the decency to slip out delicately, either. Because she'd been trying to hold it in, her laugh escaped with a loud snort. Then Eli started laughing at her, and she was lost. She laughed until the room started to darken around her.

"Hey, Mom. Mom!" Eli's voice broke through the fog and got her to stop laughing. When he came into focus, she saw he was holding out her cellphone. "Mr. Jones is on the phone for you."

She wiped the tears of laughter from her eyes and took the phone. "Good morning Mitchell! I don't have a rental car yet. Do you know anything about that?"

He cleared his throat on the other end of the phone. "It appears there was a bit of a mix-up. They went to the newspaper office to collect you. When you weren't there, they called the number on the reservation, which was my cell. They didn't reach me, so they cancelled the reservation. I called them as soon as I got the message. Someone should be by to pick you up soon."

"Okay…" Something in his voice made her ask, "Should I

be worried?"

A muffled cough came across the line before he said, "They've assured me everything will be fine, but if it's not, you're going to have to make the best of it. The admin assistant who booked the car for you said she'd used this rental agency before and that they're good for the price. I just made a couple calls to some other places to look for a Plan B, but they're all either closed for the holidays or booked up. Apparently everybody north of the fortieth parallel decided Albuquerque is the *in* place to be this Christmas." Avery could picture him reaching a finger into his collar and pulling the material away from his neck the way he did whenever he had something to say he knew wouldn't be well-received.

*Great.* "Where exactly is our reservation at anyway?"

"Uh, Mom," Eli said from the living room. "You might want to come see this."

The doorbell rang, and she moved to a side window and peeked out through the blinds. A van was here to pick them up. It had a ghastly kelly green and peanut butter brown logo. Beside it, in black and yellow, was their motto. *We Do Cars. CHEAP.*

She held her phone up to the window in order to take a picture of the offending van and in the process managed to hang up on Mitchell.

Nodding to Eli to go ahead and answer the door, she quickly sent the photo to Mitchell with a text that read, *You owe me. BIG.*

\*\*\*\*

"Uh, Mom. Are you sure this is the way?"

Avery, too, had been watching their surroundings as they presumably got closer to the rental lot. They had passed from a sunny neighborhood into one that was a little less cheerful. Then into the one with bars on the windows. Next they started to see bars on the doors and windows of homes as well as businesses. By the time Eli had spoken up, they were somewhere between the homeless shelter and the railroad tracks, not exactly Albuquerque at its best.

She'd once done a write-up on the shelter. When asking about their location, she'd been told, *"If you want to help the homeless, you need to be where they're at. That's nothing more than good business. Meet your customer where they have the greatest need. You don't sell golf clubs on a tennis court, do you?"* The woman's explanation had rung true. One question, however, had remained. After so many years, was it possible that the homeless population now came to the area because the shelter was there rather than vice versa?

*To-ma-to, To-mah-to.*

The sign at the rental lot was as horrible as the one on the van. She hadn't heard back after she'd texted the picture to Mitchell. He was probably smart enough to know he wouldn't want to hear what she had to say at the moment. Before the van could pull into the almost-vacant rental lot, they had to wait for a man wearing one shoe and pushing a shopping cart to move out of the way.

"Mom?" Eli asked again.

She gave him what she hoped was a reassuring smile and said, "Everything's going to be fine."

"I don't think so," he said.

"Honestly, Eli. It's not the man's fault he's homeless. And I'm sure this was an affordable piece of property. That's why the rental agency is here. It's about business and the bottom line. Nothing to worry about."

He gawked at her the way he would a rhinoceros barking like a Chihuahua. "Everything is *not* going to be okay. I forgot the charger for my MP3 player."

Avery swallowed. The telltale pinpricks along her neck and cheeks told her she was blushing. Here she'd been worrying Eli was concerned because he didn't feel safe. That anxiety in his voice, however, had been all about his music. *Where did I go wrong?*

The van pulled to a stop, and the driver, who had remained quiet during the entire drive, got out and opened the sliding door for them. "I need to go pick someone else up. Haul your luggage in with you so I've got room for the next group."

Looking from the two suitcases, oversized duffel bag full of snacks, and case of bottled water back to the driver, Avery lifted her eyebrow and said, "Perhaps you could assist us?"

"I gotta go take a whiz before my next pick-up. You'll have to get your bags yourself."

Closing her eyes, Avery counted to ten. Then fifteen. Then thirty. By the time she had counted high enough to feel calm again, she opened her eyes only to see Eli had already moved their luggage into the small outbuilding and was holding the door, waiting on her.

Avery stomped her way along the dirt parking lot to where her son waited. She vowed to remember every tawdry detail of this trip so she could hold it over Mitchell's head for years to come.

An entirely insincere smile pasted on her face, Avery took a deep breath and tried to relax her shoulders as she stepped into the miniature office. "Hello," she said. "I'm Avery Weston, and I'm here to pick up a vehicle. The reservation was made by Mitchell Jones, or might be in the name of the Albuquerque Times."

"Good morning, Mrs. Weston," the short blonde behind the counter said. Avery didn't bother to correct her. Maybe it would help get the process moving along if the woman thought there was a Mr. Weston who might come knock some heads together if things didn't go smoothly.

"Unfortunately, there's been a problem with your reservation," the woman said, not looking the least bit sad about it.

"I know there was a problem. You went to the wrong place to pick me up. As a result, it's no longer morning, but rather a quarter after twelve. Nevertheless, I'm here now, and I'd prefer to collect my vehicle so I can get out of here and on the road."

"Yes, well, because you weren't where you were supposed to be this morning, we had to give your reserved vehicle away to someone else."

*She did* not *just say that, did she?*

"Okay, that's fine." *Stay calm. Don't yell. Catch more flies with honey. Blah, blah, blah.* "Then please give me another comparable vehicle."

"Well, that's the thing, see," the woman, whose glaringly pale hair *had* to come out of a bottle, said. "We don't have anything left in the SUV class."

"I'll settle for a large sedan. That's fine."

"We don't have any."

"A medium-sized sedan then."

*Don't say it. Don't you dare say it.*

"We don't have any."

Avery closed her eyes and began counting again. *One, two, three. Four, five, six. Seven, eight, nine.* She would ask the question as soon as she calmed down.

"Can you tell us what you do have?"

Her eyes popped open in time to see the blonde smiling at Eli.

"Well, young man, it so happens we have a brand new cherry-red Zeon with less than two hundred miles on it."

Avery slapped her hands over her ears as her son hooped and hollered. *If he does that fist pump thing any harder, he's going to dislocate his elbow!*

"No!" Both Eli and the blonde gaped at her as if she'd been gushing over how beautiful the company logo was. They clearly thought she'd lost all touch with reality.

"But Mrs. Weston, this is quite an upgrade for you, and

we won't charge anything extra at all." Avery was finally able to get past the reflective tinge of the woman's hair to notice the two-inch long fingernails. Each painted a different color. With designs on them. *Working here can't pay well enough for nails that extravagant, can it?*

"I understand it's an upgrade, but a Zeon is out of the question."

"Is it a convertible?" Eli asked, his eyes glowing with excitement.

"It has the removable top panel so it can be easily converted to topless."

*I'm going to throw up here and now on her office floor.*

"A Zeon is not an option. I assume you have other selections for us to choose from?" Through force of will, Avery managed to make it sound like a polite question rather than a drill sergeant's command. *What kind of woman uses the word topless when speaking to a teenage boy?*

Eli and the woman stared at her.

"What exactly are you doing with a Zeon here, anyway? This isn't a high-end car lot, if you don't mind my saying so." *Good. Get the voice back under control. Don't yell.*

The petite woman stood an inch or two taller, thrust out her chest, and put her hands on her hips. "I'll have you know, we have rental facilities in different locations across the city. We rotate vehicles between all of them, and the Zeon happens to be here today."

"Right. With less than two hundred miles on it, it got sent here to this lot. What's wrong with it?"

The woman's mouth snapped shut. Then she pivoted on her heel and stomped her way into a back room, slamming the door behind her.

"Mom, what'd you go and do that for?"

*I haven't heard that whine in his voice since he was eight years old.*

"Eli, there's no way we can fit three people and all our

luggage into a Zeon. We already had this conversation. It can't possibly come as a surprise to you that I said no."

"You're crushing my dreams. I'm going to be in therapy for decades because of this, you know that, don't you?"

"That's fine. Do me a favor, though, and wait till you're paying for your own insurance before you have the mental breakdown, okay?"

He rolled his eyes at her and then threw himself into the one chair in the small waiting area. The drama of his little fit was ruined when, with a loud snap, the chair leaned drunkenly to the side. Eli's momentum forced the chair's tipped pose into an all-out flip, landing him on the floor with the chair above him, pinning him into place.

*How on earth did it manage to flip over like that? Without hitting a light fixture?*

The back door opened, and the woman returned. Her hair was the same unrealistic color as before, and her nails were still too long for her to hold a pen. *At least her chest isn't sticking out as far this time. Okay. Maybe I'm being catty now.*

With a big sigh and a lower lip that stuck out comparable to a two-year-old's pout, she said, "We have one other car that might fit your needs. Follow me."

She didn't bother waiting for her customers to accompany her. Instead, she exited out a door on her side of the office counter and was gone before they could do anything. "Stay here with the bags," Avery shouted over her shoulder as she sprinted out the door they'd come in and ran around the building trying to find the woman.

*I wouldn't put it past her to key the car and blame me for it!*

When she caught up to the woman, she scowled at the virtually vacant lot. "Okay, so where's our car?"

"There." The woman pointed. With her two-inch long fingernail.

"No, seriously. Where's our car?"

The woman's chin jutted out, and she shook a finger at

Avery. "Now see here, Mrs. Weston. You weren't where you were supposed to be, and this is the best I can do. It's either this or the Zeon. This one's at least been around the block enough times you know it works!"

Avery lifted her hands in the air and backed away. "Okay, okay. Didn't mean to ruffle any feathers. This one will be fine. I need to get on the road. As long as it runs and can seat more than two people, I'll find a way to make it work."

A few minutes later, they were back inside and filling out paperwork. She shot a quick text off to Mitchell: *I haven't heard from Gavin. Where am I supposed to pick him up? BTW, you've earned my undying promise of revenge.*

When the woman shoved the papers across the counter for her to sign, Avery scanned them. *Around the block a few times – she wasn't exaggerating!* The car had over a hundred thousand miles on it according to the paperwork. *Lord, please let that mean it's reliable. At least give me that much here.*

"Get the luggage out the door," Avery told Eli. "I'll go grab the car and bring it up here so we don't have to haul the suitcases." Then she took a deep breath and went to collect her assigned vehicle, praying it would start without any trouble.

When Avery returned to where Eli stood, she tried to force her lips into a positive grin as she got out of the car to face him. She caught sight of her reflection in the office's front window. *Ugh. That looks more like the grimace of a woman in labor than it does a smile.*

Thankfully, her failed attempt at a smile was lost on her son. He couldn't take his eyes off the car. Circling, he examined it from every angle. Then he walked around it again, shaking his head. By the time he lifted his eyes to look at her, Avery's palms were sweaty, and her heart was racing.

"You got us a decade old hatchback with less room in it than the Zeon would have had. It's so old the white paint looks faded. How can white paint fade? Does this thing even have seatbelts, or does it predate them?"

"Okay, I admit it. It's awful, but we're stuck with it, so let's get the luggage loaded. We need to leave."

She got a return text from Mitchell. *Gavin's at the coffee shop on Central between Edith and Arno.*

Clicking her fingers on the phone, she sent another message. *How will I know him?*

*He's sitting outside. Grey stocking cap. With luggage.*

A short while later, Avery was pulling their car up in front of the coffee shop. *Only in Albuquerque would a coffee shop be painted the color of terra cotta and have dried chile peppers hanging from the ceiling.*

She got out of the car and gazed at the front of the coffee shop. It was the twenty-third of December, but even in New Mexico, there was no more than one man brave enough to endure the weather outside. A nip in the air had encouraged all other patrons to enjoy the indoor atmosphere of the establishment.

Avery took note of the man as she approached. He was younger than she'd expected. With the stocking cap pulled down low, she couldn't get a look at his hair to see whether or not it had any grey in it. The scruff on his cheeks and chin was black as night, however, with no indication of aging. She couldn't see his eyes behind his sunglasses, but he had an angular face, a strong chin, and... he was drinking a fruit smoothie.

A bright yellow frozen beverage. At a coffee shop. In December. *I'm going to have to make allowances for his artistic temperament. I get it. But is this necessary, God? Sticking me with a man who goes to a coffee shop and doesn't order coffee? You're laughing at me, aren't You?*

Pulling her it's-okay-if-you-don't-love-coffee smile out of storage and dusting it off before putting it on, she approached the man. She held out her hand and said, "Mitchell sent me. Ready to go?"

The man put down his blindingly bright beverage and

ran his eyes up and down her figure. His sunglasses kept his eyes concealed, but his perusal still made her uncomfortable. When he made no move to shake her hand, she began to wonder if she had the right person. "What's your name?"

"I'm Gavin," he said. "Who are you?"

Eyeing his luggage, she took note of the oversized backpack and two large hard-sided cases she assumed held camera equipment. *This has to be Gavin, but what if it's not? What if this guy murdered Gavin and stuffed him in an alleyway, then sat down in his spot to lure me into a false sense of security so he can do away with us, too, at his leisure? Homicidal tendencies might explain the yellow drink.*

Before the man had time to sneeze, Avery whipped out her cellphone, took a snapshot of him, and texted it to Mitchell. *Is this him?*

She imagined the man blinking his eyes in surprise behind his dark glasses. *Artsy isn't exactly the first word that comes to mind here.* He was wearing black jeans, a grey jacket hanging open to reveal a like-colored sweater underneath, and a grey scarf wrapped around his neck a couple times. *I thought artists wore lots of color. Guess that's what I get for assuming. He makes me think of a beatnik.*

Avery's phone chirped at her, and she glanced down at it. *Yep. That's Gavin.*

Again frowning at the man's fruity beverage, she tried to shake off the feeling of dread swirling through her stomach. Straightening her shoulders, she held out her hand for a second time and said, "Hi Gavin. I'm here to pick you up and head to Nowhere."

He cracked a smile this time and said, "Heading to Nowhere – isn't that a country song?" Then, looking behind her, he asked, "Where's Avery?"

She stole a look behind her at the white car. *What was he expecting? A limo?* She gave him a puzzled look, brows drawn together, and said, "I'm Avery. Avery Weston."

Gavin jumped up out of his wrought-iron chair, knocking it back. "You can't be. Avery's a man."

Avery scratched her head and said, "I've been accused of a lot of things, but that's not one of them."

He turned the tables on her then, taking her picture with his phone, presumably to verify her identity with Mitchell.

Eli, evidently tired of waiting in the cramped confines of the car, climbed out and said, "What's the holdup? At this rate we won't make it to Nowhere till two in the morning. Come on, people, daylight's burning!"

Gavin glanced from her to Eli. Then his phone vibrated, and he peered down at it. The part of his face she could see through the pseudo-beard flushed. His hand clenched around the phone in a death grip before relaxing.

"I don't travel with women. I thought I was riding with a man named Avery and his teenage son."

Eli's eyebrows shot up. "You thought Mom was a man? That's awesome. Wait till I tell Grandma and Grandpa! They're going to love it!"

Avery watched as Eli immediately began texting. *Great. Now I'm a topic of gossip between my son and parents.*

She returned her gaze to Gavin and said, "Sorry. I'm not a man. We still have a job to do, though, and we need to get going. If you're going to refuse, tell me now so I can leave without you. I'm sure between the two of us, Eli and I can get plenty of pictures with our cellphones. We'll gladly give you all the credit for the shots when the article runs."

His jaw clenched.

*Maybe I shouldn't poke an angry bear.*

"It's nothing personal, but I don't travel with women."

"Why? If you think I'm going to be a bad driver, you're welcome to take your turn behind the wheel."

"I've had way too much trouble in my life with women thinking they could get a leg-up in their career by warming my bed, so I made it a rule. I don't travel with women.

Period."

*Of all the condescending, chauvinist, egotistical things to say...* Avery's foot began to tap out a harsh staccato beat on the sidewalk as she crossed her arms. Her temperature went from cool to frigid faster than a flea jumps. "One, I'm not some sweet thing hanging on your every word, and you'd best not forget it. Two, you will watch what you say in front of my son. Three..."

Gavin raised his hands and shook his head. "I'm sorry. That came out wrong. I—I'm a little edgy I guess. Can we forget I said that?" Then he glanced over to where Eli leaned against the car and back at her before adding, "But for the record, it's not like he's four years old here."

Her jaw clenched. She glowered at him for a good long minute before she jerked her chin in the direction of the car and said, "Load your equipment up, and we'll get out of here."

Eli opened the hatchback and Gavin considered the small amount of space remaining for his equipment before saying, "There's no way this is going to work."

Avery started drumming her nails on the rooftop of the car. "This is as good as it gets. They gave away every other vehicle. Make it work, even if you have to take up part of the back seat."

Not even a token protest came from Eli as the bag of snacks and Avery's suitcase got shoved up into the seat next to him. Some careful rearranging allowed Gavin to cram everything else into the tiny space called a trunk.

Eli, watching with interest, pointed to a gauge on one of Gavin's camera cases and asked, "What's that for?"

"It's called a dry box," the photographer answered. "It's designed to control and monitor humidity inside the case."

Eyebrows raised, Eli asked, "What for?"

"Changes in temperature and humidity cause condensation in the lenses and can lead to fungus and other problems."

"Aren't cameras designed to prevent that?"

Looking at Eli through the still-lifted hatchback, Gavin said, "Sure. Good equipment should be water-tight, but nothing's ever a hundred percent. Why take chances? Prevention is easy and fairly cheap compared to the alternatives."

"Huh," Eli commented before turning back around in his seat. "Who knew?"

Gavin, who had to be at least six inches taller than Avery's five-foot eight-inch frame, closed the hatchback door, and climbed into the front passenger seat. He managed to squeeze his legs into the space under the dashboard but was muttering under his breath the whole time. She thought she heard him say, "Could you have gotten a smaller car?"

"Is everything alright?" she asked, plastering a smile on her face.

"Just peachy," he replied, his tone dry.

When she pulled back out into traffic heading away from the freeway rather than toward it, he started to ask, "Where…"

"Dude," came the voice from behind them, "I forgot the charger for my MP3 player."

Avery gave her son *The Look* via the rearview mirror. "Eli, this is Mr. Eastly. His name is not *Dude*."

Gavin reached awkwardly behind him and shook Eli's hand. "You can call me Gavin, and I feel your pain."

"You have no idea," Eli said. "The rental lot wanted to give Mom a Zeon, and she refused."

"You turned down a Zeon for this hunk of junk!" Even the sunglasses couldn't hide the incredulous look on Gavin's face.

*Great. If a tire blows, it'll be because of the weight of all that extra testosterone filling up the car.*

# Chapter Four

Edgewood, NM
December 23, 4:00 p.m.

"I'm starving, Mom. We missed lunch because of the hang-up with the rental agency. Let's stop and get something to eat."

"Get something out of the snack bag, Eli. We haven't even been on the road an hour yet. It'll be sunrise before we pull into Nowhere, and I don't want to make a bunch of stops along the way to slow us down and make this drive stretch out any further than it has to."

Gavin was hungry, too, and he wasn't about to let Avery keep him from a meal. He had to admit, the fruit smoothie he'd had did *not* count as food. It was, however, far too early in their trip to start conceding victory to his traveling companion. He'd seen the way she'd inspected his drink, her lips thinned and eyes narrowed in disdain. Because of that, he planned to keep his opinion of that fruity midday snack entirely to himself. "I'm hungry, too. Mexican sounds good."

"Yeah!" from the rear seat.

"Guys, let's forge ahead. Maybe after we get a hundred miles behind us, then we'll stop."

Avery's stomach growled then. Loudly.

"Admit it, you're as hungry as the rest of us," Gavin said.

"Come on, Mom," wheedled Eli.

"Fine," she grumbled. Then she added, "I could use a pit stop, anyway."

"Mom makes *lots* of pit stops," Eli piped up. "She has a tiny bladder."

Gavin noted the blush that crept up Avery's neck and colored her cheeks. He was sure she didn't appreciate her son sharing that particular bit of information, but she didn't bite back. Instead she said, "I don't have a small bladder. I have a bladder permanently damaged from having carried and brought you into this world. You weren't exactly a small baby, you know."

Eli pointed out a sign on the side of the freeway advertising a Mexican restaurant on the corner of Walker and Edgewood 7.

An ulterior motive behind his words, Gavin casually wondered out loud, "Who puts a number in the name of a street that way?" He wanted to watch the conversation between mother and son. The interplay between the two of them was unique, to say the least.

Avery spoke first. "Albuquerque has First Street, Second Street, Third Street…"

"That's not even close to being the same thing." Eli laughed. "It sounds like a movie theater to me." Mimicking a deep theater voice, he said, "The Edgewood 7 Cinema with seven screens showing all your favorite films."

As she deftly moved through traffic and led them to the restaurant, Avery said, "You don't get to mock me, kid. I'm your mother."

"You're being crabby because you stayed up all night reading a book and didn't get enough sleep. I told you not to drink the coffee, but did you believe me when I told you it would put you in a bad mood today? No."

Gavin listened as the two Westons volleyed their conversation back and forth.

The car stopped, and Eli said, "This might not be such a good idea."

Looking at the restaurant, Gavin had to agree. The paint was peeling, there were exactly two cars in the parking lot, and he wasn't sure, but he thought some of the restaurant's windows might have peeling faded tape on them. Whether it was to cover cracks or hold the windows together, he couldn't tell.

"We passed a sign that said there's a drive-in further down the road. Should we go there instead?" Avery asked.

Gavin had the feeling Avery was used to being in charge and didn't often ask anything. He wondered if she even realized she was deferring this decision to him. "It'll be fine!" he said cheerily. "I'm sure it's better on the inside. You know how these little hole-in-the-wall places are. They usually have some of the best food."

"Then why isn't anybody here?" asked Eli.

"It's Christmas Eve *eve*. Everyone's out shopping."

"Christmas Eve *eve*?" Avery asked suspiciously.

"Sure, haven't you heard of it before?" Gavin questioned. "It's the night before Christmas Eve. People are either out shopping or too broke to eat out. That means we'll get fresh food and great service. Come on!"

It took a little work, but they all did manage to climb out of the small car without falling to the ground in the parking lot. Having been raised a gentleman, Gavin held the restaurant door for Avery. By the time he stepped through behind Eli, she was already out of sight. He removed his sunglasses and searched for her.

"Bathroom," was all Eli said.

"How big a baby were you, anyway?"

The teen shrugged. "My birth certificate says ten pounds, but if I've ticked her off, it can be as much as fifteen."

Gavin chuckled as he moved off in search of a hostess or waiter. "Hello? Anybody here?"

The man who came out from the back had food stains on his shirt, some refried beans stuck to his beard, and teeth that shined oddly when he smiled at them in greeting. After he seated them and moved away, Eli asked, "Were his teeth gold?"

Trying to think of a good way to get them out of the restaurant without having to admit he may have been wrong to insist they eat there, Gavin barely heard him. Before he could come up with a good plan, Avery slid into the booth next to her son and picked up a menu.

"Did you ask the waitress what's good here?" she asked as she scanned the menu.

"Not exactly," Gavin answered.

As Avery perused her menu, Gavin studied her. She was wearing comfortable jeans and a long-sleeved olive green shirt. Wrapped around her neck, a knitted scarf that should have looked old-fashioned complimented her outfit and set off the green in her eyes. *No, wait. They're brown.*

Gavin blinked, rubbed his eyes, and looked again. *Green.* It was almost as if her eyes couldn't make up their mind which color they wanted to be. He wondered if they changed with her mood. If so, her mood was skipping faster than a flat rock on a still pond.

Gavin had read enough of Avery's work for the newspaper to have formed an impression. He'd always thought she was a good writer but had sometimes found her approach to certain topics a little unusual for a man. Now that he could see Avery was most definitely not a man, he needed to reevaluate the opinion he'd formed of her.

A woman approached their table. She wasn't covered in food stains, but Gavin winced when he saw her bare feet.

Hoping neither Eli nor Avery would notice, he hurriedly said, "I'll have a Number One." He hadn't examined the menu yet, but there was no way to admit that without confessing that he'd spent the entire time studying the woman across from him, which he was loath to do.

"I'll have the chicken chimichanga," Avery said politely.

"The taco platter, please," Eli said when the waitress looked at him. "Could we get some chips and salsa, too? With, like, five extra little bowl-things of salsa?"

His face must have given away his surprise. As soon as the waitress left, Avery leaned partway across the table and said in a stage whisper, "Trust me, we'll go through it all. I tried to teach Eli it's kinder to make the waitress get it all up front instead of making her run back and forth to the kitchen to get more the entire time we're here."

"You two must enjoy your food spicy," he replied.

Avery shrugged, but Eli said, "Mom swears the only way she could get me to eat anything when I was little was to put cayenne pepper on it. I haven't seen any pictures to prove it, so I'm still not sure I believe her."

Before too much longer, the food arrived. They all gaped at their plates. Eli was the first to speak. "Well, I guess it could be worse." It wasn't so much that the food had a horrible appearance. There simply didn't seem to be a lot of color. Everything was covered in pale iceberg lettuce and chopped tomato that seemed to have been leached of its color.

Eli took his fork and scooped all the lettuce and tomato out of his three tacos. He piled it all on top of his beans which, Gavin surmised, were not going to be eaten.

Avery cleared her throat and gazed pointedly at her son, who put his fork down. "We pray at mealtimes. You're welcome to participate." Her voice was kind and matter-of-fact. Gavin respected that. Some people could be obnoxious about their faith, and other people could be too timid to speak up at all.

"That's fine," he said in answer.

Her mouth forming a soft *O*, Avery's eyes widened for a moment. Then she nodded, bowed her head, and began, "Lord, thank you for this food. We ask You to see us safely on our journey to Nowhere and back."

Eli snickered and then said, "Ow."

"Keep us all in the palm of Your hand and help us to remember the reason we celebrate Christmas," she continued. "Amen."

Gavin opened his eyes to see Eli reaching for the salsa. He dumped one entire bowl of the stuff over his Spanish rice and split two more bowls between his three tacos. Then he watched as Avery picked up a bowl and scooped the entire contents onto her chimichanga. When she reached for the last bowl, he raised an eyebrow, and her hand stilled. "Were you going to use that?" she asked, blushing again.

He looked down at his plate. Before his brain had time to process his thought, the words came out of his mouth. "What on earth did I order?"

"You got a Number One," Eli answered between bites of his salsa-drenched taco.

"Go ahead and use the salsa," he said to Avery as he continued to ogle his plate. He took a fork and started shoving the lettuce and tomato out of the way so he could see the food. Unearthing what might have been a burrito, he cut into it and peeked inside to find crab meat and some kind of fish with celery, beans, and rice. The second item on his plate was flat like a tostada, but it was covered in a red sauce scraped out of the bottom of a pan, possibly a week-old pan. Unable to identify the third item on his plate, he debated whether or not to risk a bite. It might have been a taquito... or something else entirely.

When the waitress came back to fill up their drinks, though, he said, "Three more bowls of salsa, please."

****

As they left the restaurant, Gavin offered to drive.

Avery shook her head. "I'd rather, if you don't mind. I'm not much for night driving, so I'll gladly let you take the bulk of the shifts once the sun goes down.

Before their little white hatchback had even made it all the way onto the freeway, Gavin's stomach started clenching. He broke out in a sweat as he clutched his middle. The cramping pain intensified with each little rut in the road. Gavin glared at Avery, certain she was hitting every bump and pothole on purpose. There was no way she could accidentally hit every bad spot in the road.

Eli's voice sounded hollow. "I don't feel so good."

Gavin sucked shallow breaths in through his nose, trying to minimize the movement of his diaphragm so his stomach might have a chance to settle down. Each breath, however, sent shards of pain shooting through his middle. "I'm with Eli," he managed to gasp.

Avery, who had been studiously driving with her hands at ten and two o'clock on the steering wheel, started darting her eyes between the rearview mirror where she could watch her son and the road ahead. Concern in her voice, she asked, "Do we need to stop?"

Gavin didn't hear Eli's answer, but Avery was rapidly moving toward an exit that boasted a rest area. For the briefest of moments he wondered if she'd have stopped for him. Then another cramp doubled him over, which was at best awkward in the confined space of the car, and he no longer cared why she was stopping, just as long as she *did* stop.

By the time the car came to rest in its parking spot, Gavin and Eli had their doors partway open. They both ran for the bathroom as fast as they could, impeded by crippling stomach cramps as they were.

Gavin couldn't tell which of them was whimpering the

loudest – him or Eli.

# Chapter Five

Moriarty, NM
December 23, 5:30 p.m.

Avery sat at a picnic table outside the rest area building. About twenty minutes prior, the sun had painted the sky in brilliant shades of pink, yellow, and orange. *The sky is so big here. A New Mexico sunset can't help but last forever.* Those previously brilliant colors slowly faded, and the last little bit of daylight seeped away.

Rising from her seat, Avery stretched before striding toward the car. She fought with the driver-side door and seat as she tried to get to her suitcase. When she got it wrestled to the ground outside the car, she opened it and rummaged through until she found what she was looking for. Once she was done, Avery zipped the suitcase closed again but decided against trying to force it into the back seat. Settling it on the front passenger seat instead, she managed to keep it there long enough to allow her to slam the door closed.

*Now how am I going to do this?*

She paced uncomfortably outside the door to the men's

restroom for ten minutes before knocking. When she got no response, she cracked the door open far enough to yell in, "Is everything okay?"

"If by, 'okay,' you mean, did we get food poisoning, and are we going to die from it, then, yes, everything is okay." Eli's voice was void of its usual vim and vigor.

"I brought medicine," she called through the two-inch opening she'd allowed herself. *Neither of them will thank me for invading their privacy if I walk in there.*

"What kind?" Gavin yelled.

She scrutinized the box in her hand and shouted back, "The generic of some sort of diarrhea medicine. It's a pill you take."

He hollered out, "Grab us a couple bottles of water, can you?"

Avery fetched the waters from the trunk of the hatchback and went back to the men's room door. After knocking loudly, she opened it the requisite two inches and asked, "I've got two bottles of water and the pills. What do you want me to do with them?"

When she got no answer, she shoved the door further open. "Tell me where to put these, or I'm bringing them in there myself!"

This time it was Eli who called out, "Don't even think about it! Set them on the ground outside the door!"

Shaking her head, Avery backed out of the bathroom and set the two bottles on the ground, balancing the box of pills on top of them. *Lord, please make them read the directions.*

\*\*\*\*

Avery decided to take a stroll around the grounds and dug a flashlight out of her suitcase. Hoping to kill some time, she began exploring the area. When insects chasing her light began gathering in hordes, though, she returned to the relative bug-free safety of the car. She battled with the suitcase for nearly ten minutes before she got it shoved into the rear seat, and even then she wasn't convinced it was going to stay there. After that accomplishment, she settled into the passenger seat with her tablet and tried to read a book.

Concentration, unfortunately, proved elusive. She gave up on the book and played a mindless card game.

After more than a half hour, Gavin and Eli made it back to the car. They both climbed in, and Gavin handed her the box of medicine. "You might want to keep that handy," he said. "You never know." His face was pale and waxy, his brown eyes glazed over. He'd removed his stocking cap, too, and his hair stood on end. If he'd looked anything like this when she'd met him, she would have given him directions to the homeless shelter, maybe even offered to take him there herself. Avery shook her head as she remembered feeling the need to protect her son as they'd passed near the shelter that morning. *I need to be kinder about those things.*

She twisted around in her seat to look at Eli, who seemed a little better off. His skin looked washed-out, and he was still perspiring, but his eyes were alert. "You going to make it?" she asked him.

Eli shrugged and said, "I'll live."

"Alright then, people, we've got a road calling our name!" She started the engine, but before she backed out, she had to tell them something. "You'll never guess what the name of this rest area is."

They both peered at her, but neither was willing to hazard a guess. "It's the Rattlesnake Rest Area! Wonder how it got its name?"

Avery put the car into reverse and pressed on the gas as she eased up on the clutch. The car moved, but something felt off.

"What's wrong?" Gavin asked.

"It's squishy," she answered.

"Squishy?" he asked.

"Oh no," Eli said. "Asking Mom to explain a car problem is worse than asking a toddler to explain calculus."

Avery ignored him and said, "The car feels squishy when it moves. Something's wrong." She pulled forward back into the spot. "Yep. Still squishy." Then she shut the engine off and got out. Gavin, looking reluctant, climbed out too.

"Well, there's your problem," he said to her. When she walked around to his side of the car, she saw what he was looking at. The rear passenger tire was flat. "Believe it or not, Eli, your mom's dead-on. With a flat, the car would feel *squishy* when driven."

*You don't have to say the word as if it's a communicable disease.*

Gavin sauntered around to the back of the car and opened the hatch. "We're going to need to get all the luggage out. The spare tire should be under the carpet back here."

Avery knew how to change a flat, but she was more than happy to let Gavin take the lead on this. She would contribute by helping to remove the luggage. When Gavin set his last camera case on the ground, he lifted the carpeted bottom of the hatch.

"Well, there's the doughnut," he said. "Too bad it's flat."

"No, no, no, no, no," Avery said. "You have to be wrong. Maybe it's similar to one of those rafts in airplanes where you have to pull a cord in order for it to inflate." Gavin stepped to the side, and she pulled the small tire out of the back of the car. She examined every inch of the tire then held a flashlight in her mouth as she examined the compartment from which she'd pulled it.

When she was done, she stood up ramrod straight, pulled the flashlight from her mouth, and tossed it into the back of the car. She put her hands on her hips, and narrowed her eyes at him. "So now what?"

"Hey," he said, "I didn't do it. Eli's my alibi. Accidents

happen. You don't need to act like you think it's my fault."

Avery ran a hand over her face while Eli called from the back of the car, "She stayed up all night reading. Mom's always crabby when she doesn't get enough sleep. Don't take it personally."

"Eli," she bit out the word. *I am so not in the mood for this right now.*

Then, to Gavin, she said, "If it were me and Eli, I'd call the tow truck now. Can you think of anything else we should try first?"

Gavin shook his head, "Call the tow truck, but ask if he can bring the materials to fix it here. Maybe we won't need to have it towed."

*Hey, that's not a half-bad idea. I never would have thought of that.*

\*\*\*\*

Gavin stared after her as Avery marched away and shook his head. "Your mom's used to everyone doing what she says, isn't she?"

Eli snorted. "She's been in charge of me for fifteen years now, so yeah, she's used to being the final word on everything. I meant it when I said you shouldn't take it personally."

"Where's your dad?" As soon as the words were out of his mouth, Gavin regretted them. He wouldn't want anybody asking him that question.

"He's gone."

Gavin cast a quick peek at the boy and saw him lick his lips and look away. He knew vulnerability when he saw it. He'd seen enough of it in the mirror during his lifetime. "I had no business asking. I'm sorry."

"Nah, it's okay," Eli said, some of the usual spark back in his voice. "There's more to it, but it's a long story, and Mom will come back before I'm done. If she catches me talking about it, she always assumes it's because I'm upset or hurt or that I need to," he sighed before adding in a pained voice, "*talk about it.*"

"Seems as if you two have a good relationship," Gavin said.

Avery terminated the phone call and began walking back toward them.

"She's been my mom, my dad, my tutor, and sometimes my jailer. We know each other better than most mothers and sons."

"Alright, the tow truck will be here in about an hour and will bring a replacement tire for us."

"Did you ask them to bring a replacement doughnut, too, so we can get rid of this one? We still have a lot of miles ahead of us."

Avery shook her head. "I didn't think of it. Maybe next time we stop we can find another doughnut?"

"Stop talking about food. You're making me hungry." Eli chimed in from his spot in the back seat.

"You can't possibly be hungry after what dinner did to you!" Avery's eyes were wide and green, and her voice rang with horror.

"Hey, I'm a growing boy. What can I say? Besides, I've never gotten sick from doughnuts before."

Avery went and sat down on the curb to wait for the truck.

Eli, now making conversation with Gavin, said, "There's this place out in some small town in Virginia called the Apple House. Supposed to have the best melt-in-your-mouth apple doughnuts ever. Mom needs to get Mr. Jones to assign her a story out there."

With a smile, Gavin asked, "Do you always think with your stomach?"

"I'm fifteen," the boy answered. "What do you expect?"

Gavin chuckled before following to sit beside Avery. "Do you think the guy will change the tire for us, or is he going to give it to us and make us do all the work?"

"He'll change it."

A mischievous grin lighting his face, Gavin said, "I'll bet that's going to cost the newspaper a pretty penny."

Avery smiled back, but her face was drawn. "Mitchell will thank me when I tell him how much I saved him by not having the truck tow us somewhere to get it fixed. If he doesn't, then I'll threaten to write an article about how this trip actually went instead of telling a cutesy little story about Nowhere, Oklahoma."

Gavin shook his head and stretched his legs out in front of him. "Remind me not to get on your bad side."

From where they sat, they could see Eli, and he appeared to be engrossed in the music on his MP3 player. Avery leaned a little bit closer to Gavin and said, "He knows me a little too well. I am undeniably crabby when I haven't had enough sleep. Sorry I was snappy earlier. None of this is your fault."

Glancing from her to where Eli sat, Gavin asked, "Why don't you want him to know you're apologizing?"

"I'll get around to telling him in due course. I just don't want to listen to him crow about it for the rest of tonight's drive."

Then she winked at him. Avery hadn't seemed like the winking type up to that point. For a moment he wondered if he'd misread her. Maybe it hadn't been a wink at all. Could it have been a highly isolated eye-related seizure? After careful consideration, he decided to go with wink.

Gavin laughed, liking the idea that Avery was pulling one over on her son. And that she'd let him in on it. Then he glanced over to where Eli sat and saw the teen watching them.

"We were chatting while you were on the phone with the tow truck. Eli says you've been his mom, dad, tutor, and jailer. I get the first three, but not the last one. What did he ever do to need a jailer?"

Avery glanced away and pulled her legs in, bringing her knees up and wrapping her arms around them. Her tangible discomfort at his question gave him pause. He would let it go. If she didn't answer, he'd change the subject to something else.

As he was trying to think of a different topic he could raise, Avery's quiet voice reached him.

"We've had our share of issues over the years. You're correct, though. He is a great kid. It wouldn't be fair for me to fill your head with everything he's done wrong before you've even had a chance to get to know him."

Gavin could hear the raw emotion in her voice as she said, "He's worth getting to know."

"I didn't doubt it for a second," Gavin replied, wondering if she was thinking of Eli's missing father who, it seemed, hadn't taken the time to get to know his own son.

"It's clear you're doing something reasonably well," he said. "Eli thinks the world of you, and not many mothers of teenaged sons can say that."

He noticed the blush that again snuck up to stain her cheeks. Gavin grinned to himself. Her discomfited reaction to his attention made him want to go deeper and understand her more. His mom had once told him that when a woman blushes, it's either because someone said something offensive or because she heard something she secretly wanted to hear.

Gavin was still shaking his head in surprise when the tow truck pulled into the rest area. The man who climbed out was tall and gaunt with sunken eyes and grease-stained overalls. He inspected their car for a minute and then asked, "You said this is a rental?"

Avery nodded and said, "Yes, we got it in Albuquerque."

"Where'd you go?" asked the man as he got out his jack and started walking toward the car. "It looks like you got it out of an old box of cereal or something."

Gavin hid a smile as he saw Avery's face flush. He was

pretty sure her heated cheeks weren't because the tow truck driver was saying things she secretly wanted to hear.

Deciding to intervene before the man could do anything else to offend Avery, Gavin stepped in and shook the tow truck driver's hand. "We sure do appreciate you coming to help us out," he said with a wide smile. "Any chance while you're here that you could air up our doughnut, too, so we have a spare in case any of the other tires go flat while we're on the road?"

The man, whose overalls said his name was *Bob*, scratched his head as he looked from Gavin to the car. "Sure, I can do that. If we had a rental agency in Moriarty, I'd tell you to trade this baby in for something a little sturdier. As it is, you're out of luck."

Bob got the tire changed in short order. While it was still up on the jack, he snagged the doughnut and filled it with air. The air hissed as it immediately leaked back out. "Valve stem's shot," he said. "If it was a hole, I could patch it. Not anything I can do about a valve stem with the equipment I've got. Sorry 'bout that. Might want to stop somewhere along the way and get a replacement. Or take it up with your rental agency."

Avery crossed her arms and planted her feet. Gavin had a feeling it was a good thing the rental agency was closed at the moment. If they weren't, he was pretty sure they'd be getting an earful from Avery.

As Bob lowered the car back to the ground, everything was going smoothly until the last couple inches. The jack slipped, and the car hit the ground with a *thud*. Then the rear bumper fell off with a hollow *plink*.

Bob scratched his head again. "I've never seen that happen before." He stepped closer and, in the glow cast by the tow-truck's headlights, gawked at the bumper without touching it. "Huh. Will you lookie there."

Gavin, unable to resist, had to see what held Bob's

attention. He, too, leaned in. "That's not what I think it is. Is it?"

Avery, who had barely sat down on the curb next to Eli, jumped up and asked, "What is it?"

Bob let out a low whistle. "You sure you didn't get this car out of a cereal box?"

Eli's voice came from the side of the car. "Is that duct tape? And… paper clips?" His disbelief was evident. "Our bumper was being held in place by really big paper clips and duct tape?" When nobody said anything, he went back to the curb and took his seat. "Mom, you do realize you gave up a Zeon for this car, right?"

Gavin bit back a smile. "Do you think we should try to put it back on?"

Avery shook her head. "If we put it on, we run the risk of it falling off while we're driving down the road."

Bob made a choking sound. "You can't exactly fit it in the car and haul it with you, you know." His eyes shifted from the bumper to their piled luggage, then back again.

Avery cast her eyes around the darkened rest area and then said, "Maybe if we put it behind the garbage dumpster, it'll still be here when we pass back through on our return trip."

Gavin thought he had a better idea. "Bob, do you think you could hold onto it for us? We can pick it up on our trip back to Albuquerque. If we don't get it from you within a week, you can toss it. I'm sure the newspaper will reimburse you for keeping it."

Bob leaned in real close to examine the bumper where it lay on the asphalt. "Seeing what shape that little car is in by the time you come back this way will be payment enough. No money needed." Then he picked up the bumper and put it behind the bench seat in his tow truck. "You folks need anything else?"

"No, I think we're good," Gavin said. "You mind sticking

around until we've got the car started up? In case something else goes wrong?"

Bob waved and climbed into his tow truck. The door slammed loudly but not quickly enough to hide the sound of the gaunt man's uproarious laughter.

Gavin scanned the pile made by his camera equipment cases and their luggage. "Alright Weston family! Let's get everything loaded up. Avery, would you prefer I drive?"

He reached out a hand to grab the keys as they arced through the air in the general direction of his head.

Once everything was in place and they were all belted in, Gavin put the key in the ignition and turned. He let out a *whoop* when the engine started with nothing more than the smallest stutter. Reaching a hand out through the open window, he waved to Bob as they passed the tow truck on their way to the I-40 onramp.

# Chapter Six

Santa Rosa, NM
December 23, 9:00 p.m.

Avery was glad when she saw a sign indicating Santa Rosa wasn't too far away. "Do you think we should stop and get gas?"

"Let's go at least another hour, push on to the next town. What do you think?"

"I think stopping for a bit sounds good." *He's not going to pick up on subtle, is he?*

Gavin peered over at her and frowned.

"I need a restroom."

His eyes widened, and his head bobbed. "Got it. We'll stop in Santa Rosa and get gas. But, for the record, we were just at a rest area." She narrowed her eyes. He bit back a smile, but not before she caught a glimpse of it.

Eli, reading a book and listening to music, was caught up in his own little world.

Avery wondered about the man sitting next to her. He was nice enough, even kind of charming sometimes. "So whatever made you decide you wanted to work for the Albuquerque Times? We're not exactly the biggest fish in the sea."

Gavin shrugged and said, "Mitchell made me an offer I couldn't refuse."

Shifting around in her seat, Avery maneuvered until she was comfortable and could watch Gavin more easily as they conversed. "Mitchell's good at figuring out what it is people need and then using that to get his own way. What did he offer you?"

"Freedom and money."

She chuckled. "That conjures up all kinds of images. You'll need to be more specific."

Gavin shrugged. "Getting back to work became imperative, but I wasn't ready to be tied down. Mitchell gave me a chance to act similar to a freelance photographer. I get to take the pictures I want when I want and submit them to him. He decides which ones fit the feel of his paper and assigns journalists to write the pieces that will showcase the photographic work. And every now and then he gives me a call and tells me something specific he needs me to cover, and I make a point to accommodate him. I'm tethered to the paper but still get to feel as if I'm doing my own thing."

Avery nodded and said, "That's a pretty unusual arrangement."

Gavin slipped a finger inside the collar of his shirt and tugged. "We're kind of family. He's doing me a favor, and I'm trying to return the favor by bringing the kind of photography to the Times that will get it some national recognition."

She wanted to dig for more answers. Instead, she said, "Mitchell's a good man. He runs a tight ship at the paper, but nobody minds. Everyone there knows he'd bend over backward to help them if they ever needed it. He has the loyalty of every staff member, and so people bring their A-game every day. Nobody wants to let him down."

Avery tried not to take it personally when it looked as though Gavin wasn't going to say anything. She was about to turn around to face forward again when he spoke. "My father was married to someone else when he got my mom pregnant. It's a big dirty family secret. He's still married to the same woman, and he's never acknowledged I exist. I don't know whether or not his wife knows."

"Oh," was all Avery could think to say. She could relate to this. Eli's father hadn't been married when she got pregnant with Eli, but he had disappeared, leaving her son without a dad. "I'm sorry. From a mom's perspective, I know how hard it is to watch your son grow up without a father figure."

Gavin grimaced. "I was the result of a mid-life crisis. He has three other children, all older than me. Two boys and a girl. The boys refuse to acknowledge me. Maybe they see me as competition for their inheritance. I don't know. When his daughter found out about me, she hired an investigator to find me. That was about ten years ago. We didn't grow up together, and she's fifteen years older than me, but I think of her as a sister."

"She sounds like someone special. It doubtless would have been easy to look the other way and pretend she didn't know there was an illegitimate sibling out there somewhere."

His eyes remained on the road, but Gavin's opinion of his sister nonetheless shone on his face. "Yeah, she's something special."

Avery studied him in the dim interior of the car. There were layers to Gavin she hadn't first seen. In a matter of minutes, she'd seen joy, sadness, pain, rejection, and love pass across his face. It wasn't always easy to find a man who could talk openly, even when it made him vulnerable.

She reached for her bottle of water and took a long drink. She saw Gavin take a deep breath.

"Mitchell's my brother-in-law."

Avery spit a mouthful of water out, spraying herself, the

gearshift and Gavin.

To his credit, other than a quick glance in her direction, he kept his eyes on the road. When she got her breath back, she said, "You have impeccable timing."

He chuckled and said, "Good thing we're stopping soon. If you're going to make a habit of that, I think I'll stock up on paper towels."

****

As he pulled the car to a stop by the gas pump, he watched Avery bolt from it and make a mad dash for the interior of the station. The man behind the counter apparently didn't understand her. She started waving her hands through the air as though using pantomime. Eventually the man pulled out a hockey stick from under the counter and handed it to her. Yanking the stick out of his hand, she turned toward the exit then ran out the door and around the side of the building.

"What kind of problem motivates someone to attach their bathroom key to a hockey stick?" Eli's voice was incredulous. He, too, had been watching his mother's antics.

"You be my guest if you want to go ask the man," Gavin told him in reply.

"No, thanks," the teen said as he extricated himself from the back seat. "But I will go wait my turn for the hockey stick." Then he strolled off in the direction his mother had run.

Gavin topped off the tank and pulled forward into a parking spot. He locked the car and went inside to see about getting something with caffeine in it. As he was browsing the drinks in the cooler, Avery's voice came from behind him. "Coffee and brownies make the best middle-of-the-night snacks when driving."

"I usually get sunflower seeds. The constant action of spitting the shells out helps keep me awake."

"Staying up to keep you company so you don't nod off

55

isn't a problem. I'm not so good at driving during the night, though. I can do it in small stretches, but something about the headlights coming down the other side of the road – even on a freeway – makes me feel weird. I'm always afraid I'm going to veer into oncoming traffic, drawn to the headlights the way a moth is to a flame."

Gavin liked the idea of visiting with Avery during the quiet dark of the night. He had the feeling this woman held a lot of secrets and had her share of pride. Sometimes the cover of night was the best way to get someone past their pride to open up about their secrets.

He grabbed a couple boxes of brownies and a big bag of sunflower seeds. As he headed to the coffee machine, he wondered when he'd stopped thinking of Avery as the woman who was supposed to have been a man and had started thinking of her as a woman interesting enough to get to know. *Probably when she threatened to use her cellphone for pictures then put my name on them for the credit. I'll bet she would have done it, too, and gone out of her way to make all the shots blurry besides.*

Gavin carried his purchases to the front checkout. Since there was no one else in the store, he set everything down and told the man, "Just a minute."

Avery, who stood nearly mesmerized before the slushy machine, turned to face him as he approached. "You want anything to drink?" he asked her.

She smiled and said, "I'll stick to the water we brought with us. It's safer that way, in case I spit my drink out all over you again."

"That reminds me," he said before jogging away. From another aisle, he held up a roll of paper towels and said, "Victory shall be mine!" Then he added it to the collection of items by the checkout.

When Eli brought the hockey stick back, Gavin asked if he'd care for anything to drink. The teen grabbed a soda out of the cooler and added it to the pile.

"Is that going to be everything?" the cashier asked without a lick of enthusiasm in his voice.

"Yep, that's it," Gavin answered. Then, leaning on the counter as if talking to an old friend, he asked, "So tell me, why the hockey stick?"

The man behind the counter shuddered. "Got tired of fishing the key out of the toilet."

# Chapter Seven

Almost to Tucumcari, NM
December 23, 10:00 p.m.

Avery was taking her turn behind the wheel. The road was more or less deserted, so she'd offered to drive for a spell. "Looks like it's going to start sticking soon."

Snow had started to fall about fifteen minutes prior, but as they continued to drive, the flakes got bigger. She'd flipped on the windshield wipers to combat the ones landing there.

"It's a wet snow, too," said Gavin. "I don't remember seeing snow in the forecast."

"Me either," answered Avery, "but I only checked the Albuquerque forecast. Didn't think to look further east."

Gavin pulled out his phone and began working his way through the menu. "Huh," he eventually said.

"What?" Eli asked.

"I thought I'd check the weather," Gavin said, "but I can't get a signal. That's never happened along the freeway before."

"You think a tower could be out?" asked Avery.

"It's possible," Gavin said, "but if that's the case, it'll be a while before it gets fixed. It's almost Christmas Eve, and there's weather moving in. I hope nobody gets stranded out here."

Eli pulled out his phone and pushed buttons for a while. "I've got a signal, but it's weak. I don't have a weather app, either, and I don't have enough bars on my signal meter to download any new apps right now."

"No weather app?" Gavin asked, eyes wide.

"Hey, I'm fifteen. What do I care about the weather?"

"Can you turn the heat on?" Avery asked Gavin. "It's getting cold in here."

Within a couple short minutes, the temperature had plummeted. Gavin cranked the heat up to full-blast and asked Eli to hand his scarf up to him. After he snugged it around his neck, he shifted toward Avery and asked, "Do you need anything?"

"I'm fine," she said as her grip tightened on the steering wheel. "I'd like to pull my phone out, but the wind is really starting to blow, and I don't want to take my hands off the wheel."

"Okay..." he said.

"Um. Uh. It's right there in my pocket," she said, twisting her hip slightly. "Do you think you can reach around the seatbelt and get it?"

Her eyes were on the road, and the interior of the car was dark. Even so, she couldn't miss the way Gavin's eyes widened as he first eyed her face then her front pants pocket.

"Okay," he eventually said. "But remember, you asked."

Avery almost laughed at how awkward he sounded. Gavin Eastly, world-famous photographer, shy. No one would ever believe her. As his fingers tucked into the lip of her pocket, she asked, "You never did much with fashion photography, did you?"

"No way," he said. "I still work with models occasionally for isolated shoots, but I never could have made it in the fashion world."

"Why not?" she asked as his fingers gripped her phone.

The phone slipped out of her pocket, and Gavin moved back to his side of the car. Avery was puzzling over why that bothered her when he said, "I have some great friends who are models. They're wonderful people. But then you have the ones who are willing to do anything to get ahead – from sabotaging each other to doing some of those things you told me not to mention again in front of your son."

Gavin, a blush emphasizing his discomfort added, "I interned with a fashion photographer when I was younger. Being around that scene all the time became a struggle for me. That's a big part of what pushed me into photojournalism, which I love. There are a lot of great people in the fashion industry. It just wasn't a healthy place for me to be."

"Oh," she said. Then, changing the subject, she instructed him to hit five-seven-one. "That'll get you into the phone's menu."

"So, is that the code to unlocking all the secrets of the universe?" Gavin's voice was warm, the discomfort of a moment ago gone. She felt herself responding to the invitation she heard in the rumbling tone of his words.

She shrugged and said, "That phone has my life in it, so yeah, I suppose you know the code to my universe anyway."

Gavin tapped away at her phone for a bit before saying, "Uh, maybe we should have checked the weather."

"How bad can it be?" she asked, gritting her teeth as another gust of wind buffeted them across the road and visibility diminished.

"They're forecasting a whiteout over most of central Texas."

"Yeah, but we're going across the panhandle," Eli spoke up. "That's not the same as central Texas. We shouldn't run into more than a dusting of snow."

"We might have a problem," Avery said.

"What now?" Gavin and Eli asked at the same time.

"The thermostat keeps creeping up." Before she knew it, a cloud of steam erupted from under the hood. Avery swung the car over to the emergency lane on the side of the freeway and engaged her four-way blinkers. "What now?"

Gavin used her phone to call information. "I need a tow truck...Yes, I know it'll be expensive... I think this qualifies as an emergency... On the freeway... I-40 Somewhere between Santa Rosa and Tucumcari..."

"We just passed mile marker 323," said Eli.

After repeating the information to the person on the other end of the phone, Gavin said, "That's fine. Yes, I understand. Of course. Thank you."

When he hung up, he leaned his head back against the seat and sighed. Then he handed Avery her phone and began typing text after text on his own.

"I thought you didn't have service?" she asked.

Glancing up at her, he answered, "I don't at present, but as soon as I do have service, Mitchell will have no doubt what I think about the rental car he procured for us."

Avery winced. "It wasn't entirely his fault."

Gavin winked at her. "Don't worry. Mitchell knows me well enough to know I don't actually plan to cut off all his toes and turn them into a necklace I can give you for Christmas."

"On the bright side," Eli asserted, "nothing else should go wrong after this."

Avery heard Gavin groan beside her. She tossed a smile to her son and said, "How many times have I told you never to say that?"

"This is different," he argued. "I didn't say it couldn't get any worse."

"Might as well have," she answered. "Anything else goes wrong after this, and I'm blaming you." Eli rolled his eyes, and Avery spun back to Gavin. "So how long till the tow truck gets here?"

"We're not getting a tow truck," he said.

"What!"

"Guy who owns the tow truck is out of town for the holidays. But there's a guy who owns a bait shop, and he knows a thing or two about engines, so he's driving on out here to find us and see if he can fix the problem. He's bringing anti-freeze, some hoses, and a couple other things."

Skeptical, she asked, "A bait shop?"

"You know," he said. "A place that sells worms and lures to fishermen."

"And women," interjected Eli. "Don't forget fisherwomen."

Avery shook her head, "Our radiator blew, and a man who sells worms is coming to look at it?"

Gavin shrugged. "Maybe it's because we turned the heat on. Or it doesn't have enough coolant in it. Maybe it's not as bad as it sounds."

After a short pause, Avery asked, "I heard you tell information you needed a tow truck. How did you end up with a bait shop?"

"They're related somehow, and when one of them is out of town, they have calls forwarded to the other."

"I need a nap," she replied. Then a couple minutes later, she asked, "So, how much is this going to cost Mitchell?"

Gavin laughed. "Well, he's charging a fee for it being after-hours, another because it's practically a holiday, a bad-weather fee, and then parts and labor."

"Dare I ask how much labor is going to cost?"

"I didn't, so why should you?"

"Mitchell is not going to be happy about this," Avery said.

"Hey," he countered, "Corporate insisted they had to have this story. Any problems Mitchell has are going to get passed up the food chain, and it'll come down to the fact that they insisted this was a condition of taking the feature national. We were provided no contact information so we could speak to someone at Corporate directly if something adverse were to occur."

"That sounds awfully similar to lawyer speak," she said.

"I may not be a journalist, but I can be persuasive, too, when I need to be."

****

Almost an hour later, an SUV pulled over into the emergency lane behind them. "He has *got* to have a specialty lift," Eli said. "There's no way it's as high as that straight from the factory."

Eli had a point. The headlights from the SUV weren't shining through their back window. They were shining over the roof of the car. *Well, it is a short car...*

They all three climbed out of the hatchback to greet the man who had come to their rescue. *I sure hope it's a rescue, anyway.*

"Howdy, folks," said a short man with bronze skin and long black hair. He might have been Native American, but it was hard to tell in the glare from his headlights. His pronounced Texas drawl confused the image.

"I was driving, and then the thermostat started going up, and before I knew it, steam was pouring out of the engine," Avery explained.

The short man from the tall truck held out his hand and said, "Name's John. Nice to meet you."

Avery shook his hand and said, "I'm Avery. Do you think you can help us?"

He gave her a relaxed smile as if he had all the time in the world. "Pop the hood, and I'll see what I can do for you." He casually walked back to his rig and started pulling out gear, including a clamp-able work light to illuminate the engine compartment.

Not sure what to make of him, Avery peered from his retreating back to Gavin and Eli but didn't say anything.

Eli made his way over to her and put his arm around her shoulders, giving her a quick side hug. "It'll be fine, Mom. I don't have school tomorrow, and the only work you have is somewhere down this road. If he can't get this baby started, I'd say he's got enough room in his SUV to give us all a lift to the nearest motel." Then he winked at her and said, "At Mr. Jones' expense, of course."

"Mothers who love their sons don't drag them out into the desert in the middle of the night, putting them at risk of hypothermia, illness—"

"—and don't forget the danger of being eaten by wild bears," her son kindly interrupted.

Avery elbowed him lightly and said, "I'll protect you from any bears that come, but you're on your own if it's a snake."

John moseyed back over to the hatchback, mounted his light to the edge of the hood, lit up the engine, and started poking around. He studied the ground under the car and said, "No water down there, so I don't think your radiator blew." Pushing and pulling on various pieces of the engine, he added, "Your hoses all look to be in decent shape."

Then he pulled out his phone and made a call. He spoke to the person on the other end in an unfamiliar language that had a haunting cadence, while he removed the cap from the radiator. His conversation continued as he filled the reservoir with coolant and put the cap back on.

When John finally hung up, Avery asked, "Was that the man who usually drives the tow truck? Was he able to tell you what was wrong?"

He laughed for a minute before he said, "That was my wife. I was supposed to call her and tell her you weren't a band of thieving murderers lying in wait for me."

"Oh," Avery said.

"My sister drives the tow truck. I talked to her earlier. She said if the hoses and radiator were fine to tell you it's likely the thermostat. That's not something I can fix, and we don't have any place in Tucumcari that would have the part in stock. You need to keep heading on down the road until you get to a bigger town."

Avery started to interrupt with dozens of questions that begged to be asked. John lifted his eyebrows, a patient look on his face, completely derailing her anxious interrogation.

When she said nothing, he continued. "Avoid running the heater. Driving a little bit slower might help, too, although I'm not sure. Stop and let the engine cool back down at least every hour, or anytime the temperature gauge climbs up too high."

Gavin inquired, "What does the thermostat do?"

John scratched his head and gaped at them the way someone from up north looks at pickled pigs' feet. "The thermostat checks the temperature of your engine. When the thermostat says the engine has heated up to a certain point, it tells the radiator to start circulating fluid through the engine to cool it down. If the thermostat's not working, it can't tell the radiator what to do and the fluid either circulates all the time or not at all. In your case, it looks like not at all, which is a problem. It don't matter how cold it is outside, your engine will still get hot and overheat if there's no circulation."

When no one said anything in answer to his explanation, John shook his head and asked, "What brings y'all out on the road tonight of all nights in this heap of... in this car?"

"What do you mean 'tonight of all nights'?" Gavin asked.

"S'posed to be a whiteout. Worst snow storm in decades, they're sayin'."

Avery contended, "But I thought it was forecast for central Texas? We're cutting across the panhandle."

"There aren't a lot of mountains around here to block a storm. If something comes blowing in, it usually gets a lot further north than it's supposed to. You sure y'all going to be safe? Might be a good idea to find somewhere to hole up for the night."

"We have a deadline," Gavin and Avery said at the same time.

He nodded in understanding. "This is one of them TV shows where you have to overcome obstacles to win a prize at the end, isn't it?"

Avery and Gavin smirked at each other and shrugged. "Not exactly," Gavin said, "but I can see why you might think that."

John collected his equipment and returned it all to where it belonged. He came back and shook everybody's hand. As he did so, he had a strange look on his face. Finally, he started to head back toward his rig. Partway there, he swung back and asked, "You know you don't have a back bumper?"

"We know," Gavin said.

"What happened to it?"

"It fell off." Gavin's voice was matter-of-fact.

Eli piped up. "The duct tape gave out."

Avery said, "Without the duct tape, the paperclips couldn't hold it in place any longer."

"We left it with someone in Moriarty. We'll pick it up on our way back through," added Gavin.

John stared at them, mouth agape, for a minute. Then he shook his head, pivoted toward his too-tall SUV, and pulled himself up into it.

****

With Gavin driving, they were soon underway. Avery sat back, mulling over her reaction to the man sitting beside her. She normally rebelled against being the passenger. Despite her deeply ingrained independence, though, something about Gavin made her comfortable with giving up that control.

As Avery pondered her revelation, Eli asked Gavin, "Don't you know anything about cars?"

Gavin shrugged. "I know the basics, but steam from the engine is beyond my skill set. What about you? Do you know anything about cars?"

Laughing, Eli said, "If I had a better signal, I'd look up a video online telling me what to do to fix it. I thought all adults were already supposed to know those sorts of things. You know, because you grew up in the dark ages before smart phones and Internet."

Crumbling up a napkin that had been sitting on the console, Gavin tossed it back at Eli and said, "You've got a lot to learn if you want to get anywhere in life there, bucko. Telling people they look and smell as good as dinosaurs isn't going to get you too far."

Eli dodged the napkin. "Hey, I never said anything about dinosaurs. You're the one who brought them up."

Then the teen stuck his earbuds back in and tucked his blanket snugly around his body.

"It's getting colder, isn't it?" Avery asked.

Gavin nodded. "You can check the temperature on your phone if it would make you happy. Not that knowing how cold it is will make us feel any warmer."

Avery pulled out her phone and clicked away. "Didn't it almost get up to seventy earlier today?"

" Mmm-hmm," he replied.

"Well, it's in the low forties at the moment. It still says snow in central Texas, but it looks as if the cloud coverage might be moving our way."

"Tonight would be a good night for a heater. I'm losing feeling in my toes."

"On the bright side," Avery said, "we're all crammed in so closely together our body heat should be able to keep us warm."

"I have a feeling all the heat is seeping out where the

bumper used to be," Gavin said with a chuckle.

Silence fell between them, but it was comfortable. The constant tinny hum of the engine, the empty road, and the darkness surrounding them all worked together to make it, for Avery at least, a relaxing part of the drive.

Then Gavin said, "Can I ask you something?" His voice, normally rich as Swiss chocolate fondue, sounded hesitant.

Avery scrutinized Gavin for a minute before answering. "Usually when somebody asks permission to ask a question, it's because they think the other person won't want to answer."

"Maybe," he said. "You can tell me it's none of my business, and I won't mind."

"Fire away," she answered. "But I'm not making any promises."

Gavin glanced in the rearview mirror. Avery, too, took a peek back at Eli, who appeared to be sleeping. "I wondered about Eli's dad. I can usually tell by the way a kid acts, but Eli doesn't seem to have any tells. Are you divorced? A widow?"

The question hung between them for a moment. Avery reached for her water bottle and then chuckled. "This is as cold as it would be straight from the fridge." Gavin gave her a half-smile. She suspected he would let her drop the whole subject if she asked. She decided not to ask. "I was never married."

*Yes, I had a child out of wedlock. Now what are you going to do with that, Mr. Gavin Eastly?*

He nodded. "I wouldn't have guessed, but it makes sense. Thank you for telling me."

Silence stretched between them, but Avery was okay with it. Even stronger than before, she believed there was more to Gavin than what she saw on the surface. It made her increasingly curious to learn why he'd disappeared from the world of photography when he had.

Something about him made her want to back off rather

than push until he revealed more of himself. It was almost as if she saw two people in him. When she examined Gavin straight on, he seemed strong, confident, and even a touch arrogant. On the other hand, when she sought his profile, Avery saw a vulnerability that touched a place in her heart she'd long since thought had been closed off from the world.

# Chapter Eight

Between Tucumcari, NM, and Amarillo, TX
December 24, 12:30 a.m.

"The temperature's starting to climb again. We're going to have to pull over." Gavin needed a break. Steadily picking up in speed since he'd started driving, the wind had gotten strong enough that he now had to fight to keep the little hatchback on the road.

"We're still about ninety miles from Amarillo. No chance we can make it that far?" Avery's voice had a breathless quality, and her words were stretched out longer than usual.

Gavin tried to read the situation, but he couldn't tell if she was imploring him about something or if she was worried. "Even if we could drive straight through, at the rate we're going, it'll take us three hours to cover those ninety miles. Why? What's up?"

He heard Avery's sigh. "I need to use the restroom."

"Oh." Gavin brought the car to a stop on the shoulder and maneuvered in his seat so he could face her. "It's the morning of Christmas Eve. We're on the side of a freeway with limited visibility. The wind is strong, I'd say at least thirty miles an hour." The look on her face grew more urgent with each passing second, making him relent. "I always carry an emergency roll of toilet paper when I'm traveling. If you want to use it, you're more than welcome. I don't want to think about you getting lost out there, so you'll need a flashlight, too." Giving her a stern look, he said, "I still don't think this is the best location for that kind of pit stop."

"I can't wait. Give me a flashlight and TP, and I'll go."

"For all I know, we could be parked right next to a barbed-wire fence with a raging bull on the other side."

Wriggling in her seat, she said, "I'll take my chances."

Gavin reached around behind him to where his backpack was stored. He extricated the toilet paper and a flashlight and handed them to her.

She smiled. "Dare I ask why you carry emergency toilet paper?"

He shook his head. "Some things are better left to the imagination. Trust me when I say that story is one of them."

Avery shut the door quietly after she got out. The soft sound of Eli's snores filled the car. Gavin reached back into his oversized bag and pulled out a big cherry and silver UNM sweatshirt and a pair of grey sweatpants. He wasn't sure exactly how to make the offer, but he wanted to have them handy in case she needed them when she returned. It was far too cold out there to be squatting in the snow.

Ten minutes passed with no sign of Avery, and he began to worry. She could have fallen, encountered a wild animal, or gotten tangled up in barbed wire. *I should have gone with her.* With a soft snort, he whispered into the car, "Yeah. Like she would have ever allowed that."

When another five minutes passed, Gavin started rummaging through his bag, hoping to find another flashlight.

He was about to wake Eli when the door opened, and Avery climbed into the passenger seat. Her teeth were chattering. Leaving the interior light off in deference to the sleeping teen, Gavin twisted in his seat and reached over to her. He took her hands in his own. "You feel like ice," he said, as he enveloped her hands and hoped his body heat would help warm them up.

"G-oing pee in the sn-ow is *not* f-un." Her teeth were chattering so forcefully he had difficulty understanding her.

"I was getting ready to come find you. You shouldn't have been gone that long. I got worried."

"Fell d-own. Twice. In the sn-ow. You're c-orrect. It's a w-et snow. Either that, or someb-ody else had already used it for a bathr-oom." She shuddered. "Gr-oss. I don't even want t-to think about that."

"Nobody else is out here on the road. I'm sure you fell in wet snow."

"I've got snow all ov-er my jacket. My p-ants, too. Maybe even inside of th-em. I can't remember the last time I was this c-old."

Her hands started to feel a shade warmer, and Gavin let them go. "I'm going to take your scarf and jacket off," he said as he again reached out toward her in the inky darkness of the car. "I've got a sweatshirt you can put on in place of the jacket, and then I'll give you your scarf back if it's dry enough. You can't sit there in wet clothes. It won't be good for you, and if Eli finds out I let you, he'll throw things at me once he wakes up."

Avery tried to help but eventually said, "I can't get the sn-aps on my jacket. My hands are too st-iff."

"Don't worry about it. I'll get the snaps. Just promise not to slap me for trying to save your life."

"This is hardly life and death," she said. He was relieved to hear the chattering fade, making her words more distinguishable.

"Of course not," he said, grinning at her stubbornness. "We're stranded on the side of the road with spotty cell service in subzero temperatures. We have no way to get warm, no means of escape, and you're in wet clothes."

A small laugh escaped. "You're exaggerating."

He got the last snap, and she turned her back to him so he could more easily pull her jacket off. He draped it over the luggage next to Eli then reached out with the sweatshirt, tugging it down over her head and helping her to get both arms through the sleeves. When he grabbed her scarf, it felt wet and icy, so he put it with the jacket and unwound the scarf from around his own neck before handing it to her.

"You can't give me your scarf. You'll get cold now."

"I didn't spend the last fifteen minutes rolling around in the snow. I'll be fine."

He paused no more than a minute before saying, "You're going to have to take off your pants."

A squeak escape her before she said, "I think I misheard you."

Gavin handed her the sweatpants and said, "Your pants are soaked, and you said yourself, you've got snow inside them as well as on the outside. Here's a pair of sweatpants. I'll close my eyes and turn away, but you need to get into something dry."

"I'm fine, really."

"You're not fine. You're freezing, and it's cold in here. Be sensible."

"Have you continued sending rant emails to Mitchell?" Her voice was suspicious.

"Why? You want me to tell him about this?"

"I very specifically do *not* want you telling him. Nobody finds out about this, understood?" Hearing that voice, he wondered how Eli could ever dare defy his mother.

*He's one brave kid.*

"Not a word," he promised. "Although, for the record, I'm sure everyone would understand."

"No, they wouldn't. They'd take one look at you, and

understanding the situation would be the last thing on their minds. Now turn. Face the window. Close your eyes. Cover your ears. And hum."

Gavin did as he was told, but he couldn't prevent the smile stretching his mouth. Avery was awfully prim for someone so independent. He rather liked it. Not that he'd tell her so, of course.

When she said, "Okay, you can turn around," he tried to wipe the smile from his face. She handed him her soaked jeans, and he added them to the growing pile on top of the luggage.

"Does that feel better?" he asked her.

"I already feel warmer. Thank you."

"So, uh, what did you mean that once people saw me they wouldn't understand the situation?"

As he waited for her answer, he turned the engine over and pulled back out onto the freeway, hoping he'd allowed the engine enough time to cool so they would at least be able to get in another hour of driving before it overheated again.

"Next time we stop, we should check the coolant level the way John suggested." Gavin almost laughed at her blatant attempt to change the subject.

"Good idea," he replied. "Are you going to tell me what you meant?"

A hearty sigh filled the car, temporarily drowning out Eli's snores. "Anybody who looks at you will not believe I took my pants off because I was cold."

A laugh escaped him before he could stop it. "You said I'm good looking, didn't you? No, no, wait. I think you said I'm smokin' hot. I could get used to that kind of flattery," he teased.

"Full of hot air is closer to the truth."

They drove on for a while before Avery asked, "So why was it okay for you to take this trip? I mean, I know your dad's not a part of your life, but don't you have family who would have expected you for Christmas?"

He shook his head. "My mom was a late-in-life surprise to her parents. They passed away when I was still in high school. No aunts or uncles." Then he wheeled around to face her and asked, "What about you? Aren't your parents upset not to have you and Eli there for Christmas?"

Avery shook her head. "They understand my job and have gotten used to me picking different days. We'll have our family Christmas on the twenty-seventh or twenty-eighth instead."

Next, she asked the question he'd been dreading. "What about your mom?"

It was an innocent question, but Gavin's insides twisted up. If he told her even a little bit of the answer, she'd ask for more, and he wasn't sure he could tell her the rest of the story without the pain washing over him. He did his best to control his voice as he answered.

"She's dead."

# Chapter Nine

Amarillo, TX
December 24, 5:30 a.m.

After a short nap during the last hour of the drive, Avery was raring to go. "Let me drive. You should get some rest."

"Look for a place to pull over. We'll get some gas, maybe find somewhere warm to get a bite to eat, and see if we can find anyone willing to take a look at the thermostat. It would be nice to drive the speed limit for a change."

She peeked at her watch and said, "Wow. It's Christmas Eve. We'd already be in Nowhere if it weren't for all the trouble we've had." Releasing a breath of frustration, she noticed the windshield. "How can you see anything?"

"Uh..."

"Gavin? How can you see anything?"

"It's not that bad, and the road's been pretty much abandoned."

"I can't see anything! The windshield is completely fogged!"

"John told us not to run the heater, and I figured that

included the defroster."

"So you've been driving like this for the past hour? Why didn't the window fog up earlier? It was clear the last I noticed."

Gavin shrugged, his hands clenching the steering wheel. "I think as long as the temperature inside stayed about the same as the temperature outside, it didn't fog up. There's been a change in the last hour, though. The car seems to have warmed up."

"Or it's gotten so much colder outside that it seems warm in here by comparison." Avery started rolling her window down. The blast of arctic air woke Eli.

"What on earth?" he sputtered. "Why is it so cold? Are we there yet?" Then, "Uh, Mom. Why are your pants back here?"

"Help me, Eli," Avery said. "We need to find the off-ramp so we can leave the freeway and get into Amarillo."

"Are you going to tell me about the pants?"

"Later. Help me find the off-ramp."

"Please tell me you're wearing clothes."

"Yes! I'm wearing clothes! Now help me find the off-ramp so we can guide Gavin off the freeway. In case you haven't noticed, we can't see out the windshield!"

"Has the snow been coming down this hard all night?" Eli asked as he peered out the window.

Gavin answered, "It's gotten heavier in the last half hour."

"There!" Eli pointed out the window.

Avery spoke up. "About fifty feet ahead... Veer to the right... You're on the off-ramp now."

Gavin laughed, "I can still sort of see. I'm not completely blind, you know."

"I need to use the bathroom," Eli proclaimed. "Can we stop somewhere?"

"That's the plan."

Avery saw the glowing sign of a gas station and directed Gavin toward it.

He didn't bother stopping by the pumps, opting instead to head straight for a parking spot. "Everybody out! Let's use the bathroom and see if the cashier can help us find someone to look at the thermostat on Christmas Eve."

Nobody had to be told twice. As a group, they collectively rushed toward the front door of the gas station and the promise of a working furnace. Avery and Eli made a beeline for the bathrooms while Gavin went straight for the coffee.

When Avery came out of the bathroom, Gavin was sitting by the front window. There were two small tables there with chairs around them. "Go ahead and get yourself some coffee," he said. "Someone's on the way to take a look at the car. If you don't mind cereal, doughnuts, or breakfast burritos heated in the microwave, we might as well eat breakfast here while we're waiting."

"How'd you find a mechanic so fast?"

Gavin stretched his legs out in front of him and leaned back in his chair. His eyes at half-mast, he said, "I have my ways."

Avery stole a look at the cashier and noticed for the first time that, instead of a burly, middle-aged man, the cashier was a twenty-something, blonde girl. "You flirted your way to a mechanic?"

"Is that why your pants are in the back seat?" Eli asked. "You were *flirting*?"

Gavin sprayed coffee all over the table as he tried to stop himself from laughing.

Eli grabbed some napkins. "Sorry, man."

"No, no. It's okay. Honestly. The look on your mom's face was worth it."

Avery glared at them both, then, face flaming, marched off toward the small breakfast food aisle.

"This would be a good time to stay on your mother's good side, Eli. Remember that."

She heard Gavin behind her, telling Eli to get a drink and something to eat.

Shaking her head, Avery brought her large coffee and chocolate-frosted, chocolate doughnut to the cashier, where she waited for Eli. When he settled an orange juice and a Jalapeño breakfast burrito on the counter next to her items, she cringed. "How can you eat anything even remotely resembling Mexican food after last night?"

He shrugged and said, "Hey, if they had jalapeño doughnuts, I'd be all over it."

Leaning close to her son, she told him, "I had to use the restroom, but there wasn't one nearby, so we stopped on the side of the road. I got covered in snow, and Gavin thought I should avoid hypothermia by changing into something dry."

Eli shrugged and said, "You could have said so, you know. It's when you avoid my questions that I get suspicious."

Realizing her son was parroting a lecture she'd given him many times, she paid for everything and went to sit down. She nodded to Eli once he joined her, and he bowed his head to bless the meal. "Thank you, God, for getting us safely this far. Please don't let the car blow up while we're in it. Amen."

"Did you already eat something?" Avery asked Gavin.

He shook his head and said, "I wanted to tell you about the mechanic first. And I think I'm still feeling the effects of last night's dinner." Taking quick note of Eli's burrito, he averted his gaze.

Nodding in the direction of the cash register, he said, "The cashier's brother's father-in-law owns a small auto shop. She put a call in to her brother. He wasn't too happy about being woken up, but he called his father-in-law, who's always up early and has a soft spot for wayward travelers stranded at the gas station where his son-in-law's sister works."

Avery lifted an eyebrow as she took a bite of her

doughnut.

"Or something along that line," Gavin added with a wink.

Eli swallowed the last bite of his burrito and said, "So I was kind of in and out of sleep last night. Totally missed the part where Mom took her pants off."

*Could he say it any louder?*

"But I heard you say your mom passed away. I'm real sorry to hear that. How long has it been?"

Avery's mouth dropped open. *Leave it to a teenager to ask the questions we adults are too sensitive to voice.*

Gavin paused for a minute. He stared at his hands. His shoulders drooped and curved forward almost imperceptibly. *This is hard for him to talk about.* She'd figured as much last night in the cover of darkness, but, somehow, seeing his reaction in the light of day made his pain all the more tangible.

"She passed away in February."

"Oh." Avery and Eli said the single word together.

"This is your first Christmas without her, and you got stuck spending it with us? I am so, so sorry." Flustered, she rushed to add, "I mean, I'm sorry for your loss, not that you're here with us. Although I'm sorry this trip has turned into such a disaster, too. I mean… I'm just…"

Gavin tried to smile, but it came across as a wince. With a sigh, Avery reached out and rested her hand on his forearm. "Gavin, I'm sorry. I had no idea."

He shrugged and stood up. Pushing his chair in, he said, "I think I'll go get something to eat now."

Eli's eyes were wide. "I'm sorry, Mom. I didn't know."

"It's okay, kiddo." How true the words. In that moment, her son did look a lot more like a kid than the young man he'd come to resemble more and more lately. "You couldn't have known."

\*\*\*\*

Gavin stood in front of the pre-packaged pastries. Cinnamon rolls. Pound cake. The more he ogled the food choices, the more his stomach rebelled. Last night's dinner, however, was not causing the problem. An as yet unnamed emotion he'd become familiar with in the past months was the culprit. He wanted to run. He wanted to hop on a motorcycle and get out of this place, leave Avery, Eli, and their familial happiness behind. Instead, he stood there in front of the artery-hardening pastry offerings and breathed deeply.

"I'm sorry, Gavin." Eli's voice came from his left. He nodded his acknowledgement to the teen. As soon as he did, Eli gazed down at his feet. Then he said, "I—I didn't know. And I'm an idiot."

Gavin grinned, hearing uncertainly in the boy's voice for the first time since he'd met him yesterday afternoon. "It's okay, Eli. You didn't say anything wrong. The Christmas season is proving to be kind of hard for me. That's nobody's fault."

Eli shuffled his feet, picked up a roll of coconut-covered mini doughnuts, put them back, reached for some pink concoction, then let his hand drop to his side. Without looking at Gavin, he asked, "Does being around me and my mom make it harder? I don't know what I'd do if I lost her, except probably avoid everyone who still had a mother."

A sigh escaped Gavin. "You're wise for your years, Eli," he said. He resisted the urge to rub at the ache in the center of his chest. His eyes burned, and he looked away as he tried to keep the tears in check. "I'm sad." With a derisive snort he said, "Sad doesn't even scratch the surface of how I feel about losing my mom." The back of his throat felt scratchy and raw, but he continued, "Yeah, sometimes it's hard to see you and your mom happy, healthy, and together, but I'm not a monster. I'd never begrudge you the time you have with her or wish you the same pain I've been dealing with these past months."

"What about your dad?" the boy asked.

Gavin offered a half-smile, swallowing down the strong emotions that threatened to spill over. "He's not a part of my life. My mom raised me by herself."

Eli didn't look as if he was going anywhere. Gavin suspected the boy had questions he didn't know how to ask, or maybe didn't know if he should. By focusing on what Eli needed, Gavin was able to keep his own feelings from overwhelming him. He pictured himself putting his grief and sadness back into a little wooden box and placing the lid on it. The grief would come again, but now wasn't the time or place.

The ache in his chest abated, and he was no longer fighting tears. "If you have questions, you can ask me."

The teen glanced up and studied him for a minute before saying, "I don't know what I'll do if I ever lose my mom." Looking uncomfortable, he added, "I suppose it'll happen someday, but…" Eli's words trailed off as though the thought itself were too difficult to voice.

Gavin put his hand on the boy's shoulder, gave him a firm squeeze, and said, "You'll man-up and find a way to deal with it. You'll rely on God to see you through the dark days." He wondered how honest he should be with the boy. "And in those moments when none of that works, you will grab onto the memory of your mother and all she ever hoped, wanted, and dreamed for you. You will dig deep and, and no matter how much it hurts, you will do everything you can to honor her memory and all she ever taught you."

Gavin took a deep breath before forging ahead. "You will find a way to be happy and to celebrate the life you have because anything less would shame your mom's memory and everything she sacrificed so you could have a chance. And the thought – no matter how unlikely – of shaming her will be more than you can bear. So on those days when the pain of losing her makes you feel alone, on those days when you start to pick up the phone to call her only to remember she's not there anymore… Those will be the days you find out what kind of man you are. And if you don't care for what you see when you look in the mirror on the bad days, you'll always know that you have the chance to change, that you can make choices to be a better man than you think you are."

Eli nodded and made eye contact. Gavin half-expected him to skitter away. If he wasn't mistaken, though, the boy stood a little taller as he walked toward the soda fountain. He could remember how it felt to be in that place between child and man with no one to guide you but your mother and friends. Gavin hoped Eli made better choices than he had at that age. Friends at school weren't always the best models for how a man ought to live his life.

****

Avery watched her son and Gavin speaking and wondered what they were talking about. *Okay, so I want to eavesdrop, and if this convenience store were at all built for stealth, that's exactly what I'd be doing right now, too.* She shook her head. While tempting, eavesdropping would go against everything she was trying to teach her son about how to live his life. *Yeah, but I still want to.*

As she took another sip of her coffee, the front door opened and a trim man in his mid-forties entered, accompanied by a woman, presumably his wife, who, if appearance could be trusted, had been woken and dragged out of bed. The woman caught a glimpse of Avery and strolled over to her. "You must be the one whose car broke down." Holding out her hand, she said, "I'm Mavis Mueller. My husband," she said, hooking a thumb over her shoulder, "is going to take a look at the engine for you."

"Oh," Avery said, the fatigue of the night catching up with her.

Mavis sat down and said, "Don't you worry about a

thing! I'm a talker. Everyone says so. You look plumb beat. No wonder you can't think of anything to say. Do you need more coffee? I can get you some more if that would make you happy."

Avery shook her head as her eyes followed Gavin and Eli. They were heading outside with Mavis' husband. Battling the fatigue that now felt mind-numbing, she forced her eyes back to the woman sitting with her.

"You poor, poor people. Stranded with a bad rental car on Christmas Eve. I hope you file a complaint with the rental agency whenever you get where you're going. The way people conduct business these days is just disgraceful. They had to know there was a whiteout coming, and here in Texas of all places. I mean, we get a dusting of snow most years, sure, but this kind of weather? It's been ages since I've seen anything as bad as this is supposed to get."

Mavis stopped talking long enough to take a sip of her own coffee, which she'd brought into the station with her in a travel mug. *She didn't seen the sign that said "No outside food or beverage," did she?*

"My husband, his name's Leon by the way, will get you fixed up right as rain. He runs a small garage on the outskirts of town. Don't get a lot of business, but that's okay with him. It's enough to pay the bills. He used to be an Air Force mechanic. Loved it. Would have stayed in the service forever if he hadn't felt God calling him into the ministry."

Mavis paused long enough to breathe before continuing. "I kind of miss being an Air Force wife. Meeting new people has always been fun, so moving around from base to base never bothered me. I wasn't all-fired crazy about it when he got deployed. I'd get mighty lonesome without him. The kids kept me company, though, and they were my kids, so they got stuck listening to me when I wanted to talk. Until they got older. Then they got real good at *not* listening to me." Mavis laughed at her own joke, and Avery took another drink. "In the long run, I think being stuck with me for a mom served them well. Each of them has grown up to be a great listener."

Avery's eyes wandered to where the men and Eli were clustered around the front of their pathetic little travel car. Leon was using hand gestures, and Gavin was nodding. Eli stood there, hands tucked into his pockets, huddled into his jacket. If she had to wager a guess, she'd say he was out there not because he wanted to learn about engines. but rather because he'd seen Mavis and decided the cold outside would be preferable.

The quiet caught her attention, and Avery spun back to the woman in question. Mavis had a content expression on her face as she sat quietly. Avery's surprise must have shown on her face. Mavis leaned in and said, "I know I can overwhelm people sometimes. It's okay. I do know how to be quiet when it's called for. Sometimes I need a reminder is all."

Avery smiled. She'd not even noticed the kindness in the woman's eyes. When Mavis had sat down and started talking, Avery had shut her out, not giving her a chance.

"Not much of a talker, are you?" Mavis asked.

"I'm a journalist," she said. "I tend to communicate better with writing. I can be pushy and blunt when I talk to people. Not everyone likes that."

Mavis chortled. "Well, then, I guess I should be thankful you opted for silence when I started in."

Avery chuckled.

"So where y'all headed, if you don't mind me askin'?"

"We have an assignment in Nowhere, Oklahoma."

"Nowhere?"

"Nowhere," Avery confirmed.

"We went through there once years ago. Not much there unless something's changed."

"Our editor made all the arrangements. Supposed to be a hotel for us to stay at and everything."

Mavis nodded, "Must have grown a lot since we were

there."

Avery had to ask. "So, God called your husband out of the Air Force, and now he fixes cars for a living. What happened?"

A musical laugh erupted from the petite Mavis. She had the kind of laugh that was always on the verge of surfacing. "He pastors a small church here in Amarillo. It's not very big, so he has the mechanic shop, too, to supplement his income. We'll never be wealthy, but we do okay."

Avery nodded and said. "I'm sure the congregation will grow."

Shrugging, the older woman said, "People come and go. The economy has moved a lot of families away from us and brought some new ones to us. Leon, he's a great pastor, don't get me wrong. He preaches a good message, and he loves his people. You'll find him at the hospital anytime someone's sick. It's an honor for him to officiate at funerals and weddings or give counsel when people need it. He'll never be the pastor of a large church, though, and he's fine with that."

Tilting her head to the side, Avery asked, "Why do you say that?"

"He likes to have a personal connection with everyone in his congregation. Leon wants to know what's going on in people's lives, and he wants everybody who comes into our church to know he cares about them personally. The way he sees it, God made some to be shepherds of large flocks and some to be shepherds of small flocks. He kind of likes that God has given him a small flock. If you ever saw him behind the pulpit, you'd know that's what he was born to do. People can't help but be drawn closer to God when my Leon delivers a message."

"Huh," Avery said. "I never heard it put quite that way before. I suppose some people are fond of big churches and some prefer small, too."

Mavis nodded. "What about you? Do you have a church

back where you come from?"

"We have a medium-sized church, I think. Not too big, not too small."

"With pews that are not too hard and not too soft," Mavis said with another laugh. This time Avery joined in.

The men shuffled back into the convenience store and headed straight for the coffeepot, Eli included. Avery had to smile. Her son had to be desperately cold in order to consider coffee a viable beverage. Then she saw him shift to the left and realized there was a hot cocoa machine there, too. *One of these days he's going to decide he likes coffee. I just know it.*

Gavin led the way as the men all came to join her and Mavis. They sat down at the other table and Leon declared, "I replaced the thermostat for you. It's easy enough to get to on this model. There's no good way to know for sure whether or not that's the problem without running the car and getting your engine heated up."

The lanky man with thinning sandy hair took a long draw on his coffee. "I gave Gavin here my number. You shouldn't be able to get more than thirty, maybe forty-five, minutes out of town before you'll know whether or not you've still got yourselves a problem. If you're going to do any driving in town, like stopping somewhere to get a new spare tire, then you'll know sooner. Give me a holler if the problem persists. I might not be able to fix it, but I can at least give you a ride to somewhere warm until someone can get it taken care of for you."

Avery, surprised, said, "That's nice of you, especially on Christmas Eve."

The man shrugged. "This is Texas. We do everything big. Including snowstorms and hospitality."

\*\*\*\*

Fortified by coffee and the smell of a pecan pie Mavis had

insisted on giving them, Avery took over the driving so Gavin could rest. She followed the directions Leon had given her, landing them at a large automotive warehouse. They were able to buy a replacement doughnut. Once they had it tucked securely under the floor mat in the trunk of their little white hatchback, they got back on the road.

Gavin quickly nodded off as Avery worked to navigate the unfamiliar city streets and find her way back to the freeway. The sun had started to climb, but with the cast-over sky reflecting dimly off the snow-covered street, it still felt like night.

All of a sudden, lights started flashing behind Avery. As if that wasn't enough to start her heart racing and her palms sweating, the officer flipped his siren on as well. Gavin woke with such a start that he banged his head against the ceiling of the car. No idea what she'd done wrong, Avery pulled over to the side of the road and waited for the officer to approach. She pulled out her license and ordered Gavin to dig in the glove box for the vehicle registration.

"What did you do?" he demanded, no doubt irritable from his rude awakening.

"I didn't *do* anything. I have no idea why he pulled me over."

"Mom."

"Not now, Eli. Do you have the registration yet?"

"I can't find it," Gavin answered. His tone and face tightening, he said, "You have to have done something, Avery. Police don't pull you over because you're driving an ugly car."

"Uh, Mom."

"*Not now, Eli.*" She reached in front of Gavin and began rifling through the glove box. "What did you do with the registration?"

"What? What did *I* do with the registration? You have *got* to be kidding me."

The tension in the small car quickly escalated. Avery's

heart raced, and her arms and legs ached with how tense they were. She felt jumpy from the adrenaline rush, and, to make matters worse, her bladder again told her it was time to stop.

The officer remained in his car, no doubt calling in their license plate to make sure they weren't mass murderers on the run from the gaol.

"Mom!" Eli yelled. Avery bit back her irritated response when she saw him pointing to something. Her eyes followed his finger.

"Well, that explains a lot," Gavin said.

Avery stared in disbelief.

The officer finally approached the driver's side window and tapped lightly before stepping back. Avery pushed the button to lower the window and said, "Hello, Officer. I didn't see the sign when I pulled onto the road here. I'm so sorry. I was trying to get back to I-40."

"License and registration, please."

"Aha!" Gavin shouted, waving a piece of paper through the air. "I found it!"

He handed the registration over to Avery, who handed it and her license out the window. The officer, whose nameplate said Delaney, reviewed both and called something in using the two-way radio strapped to his shoulder. Still standing away from the car, he asked, "Where you folks from?"

"Albuquerque," Avery answered. "We're heading to Nowhere, Oklahoma."

The officer's eyebrows went up. "Not much in Nowhere. Is that your final destination?"

Avery nodded. "I'm a journalist, and Gavin here is a photographer. We're on assignment for the Albuquerque Times. We've been ordered to do a Christmas story about Nowhere, and the folks at Corporate want it to be authentic, so we have to actually be there on Christmas." She rolled her eyes. "If you can believe it, we left Albuquerque yesterday around three o'clock. This car has given us nothing but trouble."

Hands clenched in her lap, Avery made herself stop talking. *Keep this up, and he'll ask if you're related to Mavis Mueller.*

A voice came back over Officer Delaney's two-way radio, but Avery couldn't make out the words.

The officer stepped closer to her open window and handed her license and the car's registration back.

"This has got to be the most miserable excuse for a rental car I've ever seen. No rear bumper, you only have one working taillight, and it looks like the three of you can barely fit in there."

He pointed over his shoulder to the sign Eli had pointed out. "I gather by now you've figured out you're going the wrong way down a one-way street." Avery nodded. Then he pointed to the building across the street from them. "Of all the roads in town to get turned around on, you chose the one in front of the police station. You never had a chance."

For the first time, Avery scanned the street around her and realized it was littered with police cars. She'd been so caught up in her own panic at being pulled over she hadn't realized where they were. Avery slapped her palm against her forehead.

"I'm an idiot," she said to the officer.

He laughed and said, "Don't worry about it. As it happens, the one-way sign where you made the left onto this road is obscured by snow."

"Thank you, Officer Delaney. You have no idea what a horrible trip this has been. Your kindness is appreciated more than you know."

Gavin spoke up from the passenger seat, "Any chance you can give us directions back to the freeway?"

He nodded and said, "You'll need to take a U-turn here. It's illegal on this street, but I'll stop the flow of traffic and wave you through."

*What traffic?*

"Once you get to the end of the block, take a left on Third and then a right on Pierce. It won't be too long till you see signs for the freeway. They're real obvious. You might want to know, though," he said, pausing, "the freeway is closed down east of here. You'll be on it for a short spell, then they'll detour you off to US-287 South."

"Why is it closed?"

"Whiteout conditions, and they haven't been able to get anyone out there yet to clear it. The snowplows are busy, and this snow keeps coming down. I'm thinkin' it'll be afternoon before they get it cleared again. Your detour will take you down through Washburn and Claude. At Claude, you'll either be directed back to the freeway or you'll be kept on the detour. It depends on the road conditions by then."

"Thank you for your help," Avery said, offering the man a smile.

He nodded and stepped away from the car and out into the road. No traffic was coming for him to stop, so he swept his arm out in the traditional traffic cop motion for *turn*, but he put a little extra twist into it, which she assumed was his signal for U-turn. Avery started the engine and did as directed. She, Gavin, and Eli all waved to Officer Delaney as they left him in their rearview mirror and once again headed toward their destination.

# Chapter Ten

Goodnight, TX
December 24, 9:30 a.m.

They made it out of Amarillo and followed the freeway until they were directed onto the detour as Officer Delaney had said. The engine was cooling, and the heater was warming. Everything was going well, and Avery was beginning to believe the worst of the trip was behind them. She dared not say it out loud, but she did let herself think it for the barest hint of a minute: *What else could conceivably go wrong?*

Gavin nodded off again, clearly exhausted. Eli was listening to his MP3 player, which he now had plugged into the car's only cigarette lighter for power. Avery, not wanting to wake Gavin, was left with her own thoughts for company.

Spending time with her own thoughts didn't always go well for Avery. She had an admitted tendency to over think situations. As she drove, she had to ask herself why they hadn't turned back the first time things started to go wrong. *Because I'm a glutton for punishment.*

When exactly should she have conceded defeat? An ugly car that looked old and was too small wasn't the end of the world. Flat tires happened to people all the time. *Yeah, but the bumper falling off... because the duct tape had given out...* Admittedly, the bumper should have been a red flag. The snow wouldn't have sent her scurrying back to the safety of Albuquerque. *People drive in bad weather all the time. We're just spoiled in the Southwest.* A failing thermostat and overheating car might have been a clue to some people. *By then we were already halfway to Nowhere. It didn't make sense to turn back. I mean, what else could have gone wrong at that point?*

The snowfall, which had been increasing as Avery had allowed her mind to contemplate their road trip, began to come down so heavily she had to turn her windshield wipers on high to keep up with the thick flakes. Following the instructions her grandmother had given her years ago, she gripped the steering wheel firmly and leaned toward the windshield to better see. *It's nothing more than weather. Stay alert, and everything will be fine.*

"Is everything okay?" Eli asked.

Gavin stirred but didn't wake.

"The snow's getting pretty heavy," she answered.

"You could always pull over and wait it out," her son offered.

"If this doesn't ease up, I might have to."

No sooner had the words left her mouth than a loud *thwack* against the windshield echoed through the car, and she lost all visibility. Avery instinctively yelled for Gavin to roll down his window.

The poor guy, who'd been asleep at most thirty minutes jumped, again hitting his head on the too-short ceiling of the car. He rubbed his head and glowered.

"Put your window down," she ordered. "I need to know where the side of the road is. We've got to pull over." Avery had her window down by then, too, and was leaning out far enough to keep an eye on the orange line of the road to at least make sure she didn't veer into the other lane. She didn't want to slow down too much in case a car came up behind them and, in the heavy snow, didn't see them. The last thing they needed was to get rear-ended.

"Okay," Gavin said. "The shoulder's plenty wide. Start to pull off toward the right. I'll let you know if you get too close to the edge, but you should cross over the white line enough to see it on your side before that ever happens."

Gavin directed her off the road and into the emergency lane. Once she had the emergency brake in place and the four-way blinkers flashing, the two of them got out to inspect the damage to the windshield.

Gavin lifted the empty metal arm that would have normally held the passenger-side windshield wiper. The wiper on the driver side of the car had come loose, too, but was still hanging on, caught on a lip of the metal mechanism. Avery rescued it and attached it firmly back into place.

"What do we do now?" she asked.

"Well, the way I see it, we have two choices." Gavin put his hands on his hips and shook his head. "We can leave it as-is and run the windshield wipers. The passenger window will get scratched up by the metal arm on this side, but then we can stop at the next town or truck stop and get a replacement wiper for it."

"Or?" she asked loudly, trying to be heard over the now howling wind.

"Or we break the arm off. This saves the windshield but costs us a later repair and means we don't have a passenger windshield wiper at all for the rest of this trip."

"I don't care for either of those options," she said in reply. "Do you have anything better to offer?"

"Not at the moment." He shook his head as he continued to study the hatchback. Then, a smile lighting his face, Gavin raised a finger into the air. "What about this? We put a sock or two on the arm, secure it tightly into place, and leave it be to run. The sock should protect the windshield. We can buy a new blade at our next stop, and the windshield will be none the worse for the wear."

"Brilliant!" she said, happy it was going to be an easier repair than she'd thought. "You're pretty quick for someone who keeps hitting his head." She winked and reached in through the open driver window. "Eli, open the side pocket on my suitcase and pull out a pair of socks."

Her son raised an eyebrow in question but did as he was told. When he pulled out a brightly colored pair of thick wool socks, she shook her head and said, "No, not those. I like that pair. Get me some socks I don't care about." Plain white cotton came out next, and she nodded. "That'll do it."

Avery tossed the socks to Gavin, who put one of them around the metal arm of the wiper and used some electrical tape from the glove compartment to secure it into place.

"You sure one will be enough?"

"We might need the other if this one blows off or comes loose."

"Alright, let's go," she said as she opened the driver-side door. Looking at the snow on her seat, she added, "I can't believe I left the window down." Avery brushed as much of the snow off the seat as she could but knew she would likely end up with a cold backside as soon as she sat down. Muttering, "I should have known better," she climbed in, rolled up the window, and started the engine.

"We have a problem," Gavin said.

"Put your window up so we can keep the cold out then tell me what the problem is."

"The window *is* the problem," he said.

Avery, her stomach lurching in sudden upset, searched Gavin's pale drawn face then eyed the button he kept pushing to get his window to go up. Only, the window wasn't moving. *What else could go wrong indeed!*

"Maybe you're pushing it wrong?" she asked.

Gavin threw the car door open, jumped out, slammed it closed behind him, and went marching off into the snow.

Avery let him go. This was turning into the worst road trip in the history of every road trip ever taken by mankind since the Model-T first came off the assembly line. She couldn't blame him for needing to walk off his frustration, which she assumed was the cause of his sudden exodus. In his absence, she couldn't stop herself from leaning over and trying the push-button switch to see if it would by some miracle work for her. *If I could be so lucky.*

"Any ideas, kid?" she asked Eli, turning the ignition back off.

"I packed an extra pillow. We can use the pillowcase and tape it into place over the opening."

"That won't keep the cold out."

"It might keep the snow out, though. If we had plastic..." His voice trailed off as he began digging around on the floor at his feet.

"Here!" Eli tossed the plastic covering from the case of bottled water she'd insisted they bring. With the plastic and my pillowcase, we should be able to block the worst of the snow and wind. It won't keep the cold out, but it'll be better than the pillowcase by itself. With the heat working, we should be fine till we can get it fixed. If the heat still wasn't working, we'd be in a lot worse shape."

Avery and Eli worked at getting the plastic and pillowcase stretched over the half-opened window and used the electrical tape from the glove compartment to seal all the edges the best they could. By the time they were done, Gavin was heading back to the car. His pants were crusted with snow all the way up to his knees, his cheeks and nose were ruddy from the cold wind, and he was chafing his hands together for warmth. Despite all that, he was calmer.

"Sorry for losing it."

Shrugging, Avery said, "Until I got pulled over in Amarillo, I was wondering if you were even human. You've been handling everything so well. I'd hardly call that little scene 'losing it,' but it's good to know you're not as perfect as you'd first seemed."

A grin broke across his face, and his eyes twinkled, "Perfect, huh? That sounds good coming from you."

She shook her head and wrinkled her nose in mock disgust. "Just get in. We should be able to find help at our next stop."

"What's our next town?" Gavin asked.

"Clarendon, I think."

"They should be big enough to have a hotel, wouldn't you say?"

Avery nodded as she pulled back onto the road. "Should be, and I can't imagine they'd all be booked up. Think we should stop?"

Gavin nodded. "We could all use some shut-eye. Even if we get no more than four or five hours before we get back on the road, I'd feel better if we were both rested so we could be awake in the car."

Avery, who'd managed about three hours of sleep during the night, was faring better than Gavin, but she had to admit, even she was starting to lose her ability to focus. Her responses were slowing, too. She finally nodded and said, "Sounds like a plan. Think there'll be an obvious one, or should we see if GPS can help?"

Gavin activated the screen on his phone and laughed, "I don't know if we still have it or not, but I must have gotten a signal at some point. All my texts to Mitchell went out." He pushed a few more buttons and said, "Clarendon's not huge, but they've got two hotels on the main road. We shouldn't be able to miss them."

The thought of sleeping rejuvenated Avery. "So much for being able to drive straight through to Nowhere. But, oh, blessed sleep, here we come!"

# Chapter Eleven

Clarendon, TX
December 24, 4:00 p.m.

A light knock came at Gavin's door. He smiled to himself before swinging it wide to admit Avery. She looked as if she'd barely woken up, and it was a look she wore well.

"Eli asleep?" he asked.

She laughed. "He got more sleep last night than anybody. You'd think he would be the one itching to get back on the road."

"I'm not sure any of us are in a hurry for that," he said.

"Yeah, but…" her voice trailed off.

Gavin waved her over to the desk chair resting in front of a table in the corner of his room. "Have a seat."

He settled in on the bed cross-legged, and said, "I called an auto-parts store before I fell asleep. The guy told me how to fix the window. Said there's no way to get it replaced around here what with the holiday and all, but fixing it should be fairly easy."

"Okay. What do we need?"

"A flat-head screwdriver and some strong adhesive duct tape. Hopefully that's all."

Avery wrinkled her brow. "I've lived my whole life without realizing how valuable duct tape is to automotive repair. How did I ever survive?"

Gavin shook his head at her, a smile lighting his eyes. "I'll need to remove the interior panel of the door – that's where the screwdriver comes in – and then I'll have to pull the window up and prop it into the closed position. I need to wedge something under it so it doesn't slide back down. Then, to get a good seal at the top, the man I spoke with said to use a good quality duct tape. That should hold it all the way to Nowhere and back to Albuquerque."

Avery nodded and bit her lower lip.

Gavin wasn't in a hurry to go stand outside, trying to make a repair he'd never attempted before, so when he thought there might be something else Avery wanted to discuss, he didn't rush her.

After a couple blinks, Avery said, "I wondered if I could ask you something about Eli."

Surprised, Gavin said, "Sure, but I think you'd have better answers than I would. You know him a lot better."

She nibbled on her lower lip again for a minute before saying, "Are you a man of faith?"

Taken aback by her question, Gavin slowly nodded and said, "Yes, I'd like to think so, but that could mean a lot of different things to a lot of different people."

Avery chewed on her lip a bit more before saying, "I'm not very good at these sorts of conversations. Give me a corrupt businessman to interview any day over a conversation about personal beliefs." Gavin waited for her to continue. She eventually made eye contact and said, "Do you believe in God?"

"I do," he replied, adding, "I believe in God the Father and salvation through His Son Jesus. Is that what you're trying to dig at?"

Avery's lips stretched into a smile, and her eyes brightened. Gavin couldn't help but grin in return when she said, "Yeah, that was pretty much what I was getting at. Like I said, I'm not very good at that sort of thing."

Gavin leaned back in his seat and relaxed, settling in for a longer conversation. "Was that all you wanted to ask, or was there something more?"

A light blush tinged Avery's cheeks. "You haven't known us long, but you've spent more time with us than most."

"Ask away," he said, wanting to ease her obvious discomfort.

"I don't understand boys all that well. I mean, I know Eli, but as he's gotten older, he's not as easy for me to read. There are some things that worry me, but I don't want to ask him. If he thinks I'm worried about it, he might try to hide it from me, you know?"

Gavin could remember going through similar struggles with his mom. "With only the two of you, it's natural to want to protect each other. The two of you against the world and all that." He nodded in understanding before adding, "Of course, that mentality may not always be best. I tend to think open honesty is the best course of action, even when you're tempted to do something else. Maybe especially then."

She shrugged and said, "When Eli was little, he would tell me everything. He doesn't so much anymore. He used to be an open book, too. I—I've been worried about his relationship with God."

Gavin's wonder grew. She must be desperate for advice to be coming to him, a virtual stranger, for something so personal.

"Eli never complains or puts up a fuss when I ask him to pray, and he goes to church without complaint, but he always seems to be fiddling with his phone when we're there. I never see him reading his Bible or trying to get involved with the youth group or doing things it seems a teen who loves God ought to be doing."

"In other words, he's not doing things exactly the same way you would do them."

Avery lifted her hands and said, "See? I don't know if I'm reading him right. I'm afraid if I keep trying to push him toward God, I'll end up pushing him away without meaning to."

"Did he used to be more active in those things?"

She nodded and said, "I worry he's going through the motions because he thinks it's expected. What if it's all just an obligation he feels he has toward me? It needs to be something that's in his heart where it can change him from the inside out. I want him to have a vibrant relationship with Jesus, but I don't see it in him. You're objective. What do you see?"

Gavin knew he needed to choose his words carefully. "I don't know Eli well enough to be able to answer your questions. From my own personal experience, though, I can tell you men express their faith differently than women. You may not see it oozing out of his pores, but that doesn't mean the boy's not filled with faith. Even as his mother, you can't know what's in his heart."

When his guest said nothing, he asked, "Are you the type of parent who helps with homework or who does the homework for their child?"

Squinting at him, she answered, "I help when he needs it. He won't learn anything if I do it for him."

Gavin maintained that eye contact and asked, "Isn't this the same? You have to allow Eli to find his own path with God, to make his own choices. You can't do the homework for him, not if you want him to get anything out of it."

Avery broke eye contact and sighed.

"You don't have to care for my answer, but I think if you want to know where Eli is in his relationship with God, you should ask him. He's the only one who can tell you what he's really thinking."

"I don't want to put him on the spot," she answered.

"From what I've observed of the relationship you two share, he won't be offended by your question, and he won't lie to you. That's my take on things, anyway. Like I said, you know him a lot better."

"He felt terrible for bringing your mom up."

It appeared she was done with the topic of her son's faith. He allowed the change in subject. After all, she was the one who'd brought it up in the first place. She ought to have the right to say when they were done talking about it.

"Eli's a good kid, Avery. You've got a lot to be proud of."

Avery's hands relaxed in her lap. She dug the toe of her shoe into the carpet and pushed her chair back and forth in a small rotation. "Can I ask you something else?"

Not bothering to hold back his smile, Gavin said, "Ask away."

"Why'd you disappear? You were a rising star in photojournalism. You were on your way to the top, but then you vanished."

Gavin felt the familiar tightening in his chest and the pinprick sensation moving across his back. "My mom got sick."

He could see the question on Avery's face, even if she was too sensitive to ask it.

"Leukemia. The diagnosis was bad. The doctors didn't give her long to live. My mom had given up her dreams to raise me. We'd always been close, but when she got sick, I knew I had to be there for her. I had some things in my life I regretted, but they were on me. They weren't things that affected other people. But this was my mom. If I bailed on her, if I couldn't handle being there and seeing her sick, I would know for the rest of my life, I'd hurt her, and if she died, it wouldn't be the kind of hurt I could ever apologize for."

Gavin ran a hand along his jawline, feeling the brush of

scruff against his palm. He peeked at Avery and saw sympathy in her gaze. Sympathy, but not pity.

"I broke all my contracts and came home to be with Mom. I moved back in, took her to all her appointments, played board games with her on her good days, read to her on her bad ones. She fought to live, and she did that for me. One of her nurses came to see me afterward. As bad as things were, she told me, most people would have been gone at least a year sooner. Mom fought to live because I asked her to. She did everything she could to stay alive because she loved me."

Tears burned and threatened to spill over. He blinked, trying to put a lid back on the emotion. "She's gone, and I miss her, but I will forever know I did all I could to help her and that I gave her the best of me in her final years. In the end, it wasn't enough, but I did everything I could."

Avery blinked rapidly and wiped at her eyes. "I think men and women handle things differently."

He stared at her, nonplussed. Hadn't he just said that, but about faith?

She chuckled. "Okay, I know. Obvious. Hear me out anyway."

He nodded for her to continue. She tugged at the scarf around her neck, the feminine one she'd been wearing when they'd first met, not his bulky one.

"When a woman sees someone she loves in pain, her natural instinct is to comfort and nurture. No matter how bad the situation is, a woman can find a way to be useful. She can ease the pain or difficulty of the situation in any number of ways."

Avery paused as if carefully choosing her words. "When a man sees someone he loves in pain, his natural instinct is to protect and defend. He puts the person he loves behind him and raises his sword and shield to fight off the enemy and keep his loved one safe." She blinked slowly as he watched her. "There are some things against which no man can defend.

I'm sure you did everything you could to protect your mother, but you were never going to be able to protect her from leukemia."

What she said made perfect sense. Gavin cocked his head to the side. "That's an interesting perspective."

Avery pulled at her scarf and dipped her chin low, breaking eye contact. "It's something I learned when I was pregnant with Eli. The way my parents handled things was... different. My dad let guilt eat away at him and get in the way of our relationship because he thought he should have protected me better. That's been years ago, and we're all fine today, but it's a lesson I've always remembered."

Wanting to break through the fog of emotion in the room, Gavin winked at her and said, "You're smarter than you look."

She shook her head and said, "That's another thing I know about men. They crack jokes when things get serious."

Rising from the bed, Gavin gave her a thoughtful look and said, "We might try to lighten the mood, but don't take that to mean we didn't hear the message."

****

Avery gazed into Gavin's intense brown eyes and thought she might melt into a puddle on the spot. *Is this what a hot flash feels like?* She held herself together enough to nod acknowledgement, but she was ever–so-thankful when he wheeled around and headed toward the door.

"I'm going to ask at the front desk and see if they have a screwdriver and some duct tape I can use. If I'm lucky, they'll let me pull the car in under the front portico out of the snow."

The mention of her fluffy white nemesis served as a cold shower. "Is it *still* snowing out there?"

"I took a glimpse out the window when I first woke. It doesn't look to be coming down much anymore, but the streets are still covered. I'm guessing everybody got overwhelmed by the magnitude of the storm."

"Especially if they believed it would stay to the south the way we did."

"According to the television, the worst of it is still staying well to the south of here, but as a result, most of the resources to help with people and roads are being sent there as well, leaving the people this far north in a bit of a bind." Gavin stood up and stretched. "Feel free to hang out here, but make sure you lock up if you leave." Then he stuck his room key in his back pocket and headed toward the door. "I'll go see what I can do to get the window fixed."

Avery nodded but stayed quiet. *What I really want is a shower, but I think I'll head back to my own room for that, thank you very much.*

Gavin had kindness in him. She could see it in his eyes and in the way he treated the people around him. He took the time to talk to people. Whether it was the mechanic, the cashier at a gas station, or the front desk clerk at a hotel – he made friends everywhere he went because he was nice to everybody and took the time to treat them as individuals. More of a straight-to-the-point person, Avery knew the niceties of conversation had never been her strong suit. She could learn a thing or two from Gavin.

But first – hot shower!

\*\*\*\*

Gavin was able to get the window secured in place much more quickly than Avery had anticipated. She was still fresh from the shower when he knocked at her door and said, "It's ready. Let's grab a bite to eat and blow this joint!"

They decided, for the sake of getting to Nowhere before midnight, they would get fast food and eat in the car.

"I'll take this stretch," Gavin said, climbing into the driver's seat. Avery, who wasn't used to being told what to do, wasn't nearly as bothered by his high-handed controlling of the situation as much as she thought she ought to be.

In short order, Eli was speaking around a bite of hamburger. "It's almost like, if we take too long... if we stop to get a bite to eat or anything, it's exactly enough time for something else to go wrong with the car."

"Don't talk with your mouth full," his mother corrected.

"And if you're going to say things like to that," Gavin added with a wince, "it might be best not to talk at all."

The nap had done Avery good. She felted rested and ready to tackle whatever else came up. *It would be nice if nothing else came up.*

# Chapter Twelve

Memphis, TX
December 24, 6:30 p.m.

As Gavin, who was driving, crumbled up the wrapper from his burger and stuffed into the empty bag between their seats, he said to Avery, "So tell me about your parents. You know a fair amount about my family. Tell me about yours."

"Grandma and Grandpa are cool," Eli said. "They got me my first cellphone!"

Avery rolled her eyes. "Can you believe it? They bought him a smart phone and put him on their plan way back before I could even afford to have one of my own. Talk about power going to a kid's head." She waggled her fingers at Eli in the rearview mirror.

Gavin studied her, an expectant look on his face. "You want the whole kit and caboodle, huh?"

"Yeah. Give me the background. Where you grew up. What they did for a living. The works."

"I grew up in Rio Rancho, north of Albuquerque. My folks still live there today in the same home where they raised me. Good, God-fearing folks. Hard-working. Best parents a girl could ask for."

"So," Gavin said, "basically the American dream?"

She laughed self-consciously. "More or less, yeah."

"What'd they do for a living?"

"My dad's a pulmonologist. My mom stayed home with me when I was growing up, but when I got older, she got a part-time job as a receptionist in a dental office."

Gavin sounded surprised when he asked, "They're still working?"

Avery nodded. "They're in their fifties. Dad still works full-time, and Mom has kept her part-time job all these years."

From her vantage point, Avery saw his eyebrows lift then relax back into place. He started tapping one of his fingers on the steering wheel. She knew he wanted to ask. *What went wrong? How'd you end up pregnant and unmarried?* The question was there on his face, but she figured he wasn't going to ask it with her son right there in the car. He'd probably say it a lot more tactfully, too.

Eli also picked up on it. With a shake of his head, the teen said, "I've asked him all kinds of personal questions. I'm pretty sure you can tell him where babies come from. Seems a trustworthy sort."

Gavin sputtered, and Avery gulped down the drink of water she'd just taken. "Eli, *really*."

He grinned unrepentantly and put his earbuds back into place.

\*\*\*\*

Gavin glanced over at Avery and saw the blush staining her cheeks. Eli sure did know how to push his mom's buttons. In his own way, he'd given her permission to tell Gavin about where he'd come from.

Returning his eyes to the road, he waited for Avery to

speak. A couple minutes passed before she began.

"I was a junior in college. I was working for the campus newspaper chasing an article about the campus ROTC programs."

"Chasing?" he asked.

From the corner of his eye, he caught her shrug. "It seemed like a big story at the time. As it turns out, in the whole scheme of things, it wasn't such a big deal. While I was on the story, I met this airman. He was smart, handsome, funny... all the things I wanted in a man." She ran her fingers through her hair and said, "All the things I thought I wanted, anyway. I was a little too young to realize that wasn't the complete package."

When she paused, he asked, "What was missing from the package?"

"Commitment, mostly. Some other things, too, but mostly commitment."

Gavin had the feeling she was leaving some parts of the story out in deference to her son, sitting a short distance behind them.

"We dated for about eight months. I fell crazy-out-of-control in love. He proposed, and I said yes. As a low-ranking second lieutenant, he didn't make a lot of money. So I was going to have to wait for a ring. I didn't mind. We were in love and engaged."

"What changed?"

She sighed. "He got his orders. Deployment was coming. I wanted to get married before he left, but he wanted to wait till he got back. This man I loved was going into harm's way and might not come back to me alive. It was overwhelming. Then he said he wanted something to remember me by. I said no, but he kept bringing it up. Eventually I said yes. I probably would have done anything he'd asked by then. I didn't want to see him go, and I believed we'd be getting married when he returned."

Gavin, fearing the worst, asked, "Did he return?"

She snorted. "He didn't die, if that's what you mean."

That was exactly what he'd meant.

"He never intended to marry me. More than one girl on that campus got played by him the exact same way. How he managed to keep us all straight is beyond me. It turned out I was the only one in his little collection who'd planned to wait till she was married to, um, get involved like that... which meant I was also the only one not already on the pill."

Gavin would have punched the guy if he'd been there. His hands clenched around the steering wheel, and he felt the muscles in his back and neck tense. Keeping his voice modulated, he said, "I'm sorry he treated you that way."

Avery shrugged. "We all have to learn the harsh realities of life eventually. I learned while I was in college. Unfortunately, that meant Eli had to learn as an infant."

"He seems to have handled it well."

"I'm blessed. He's a good kid. And I got to finish college. By the time I realized I was pregnant, I was already partway into my senior year, and the airman in question hadn't replied to any of my emails in months. I did the only thing I could at that point. I went home and told my parents."

Gavin winced. He knew she was on good terms with her parents, but that had to have been a difficult task for her to face.

"They never wavered in their love, and they never blamed me. I have amazing parents, and I know how fortunate I am in that regard." She fidgeted with her water bottle for a while before taking a drink. Then she said, "With their help, I was able to finish college and serve an internship with a local newspaper. I don't know where Eli and I would be if it hadn't been for them."

"Did you tell him he was going to be a father?"

"I did," she said. "Email, snail-mail, airmail – I tried everything I could think of until the mail started getting returned unopened. A friend of mine was dating someone in his unit, so I knew when he returned stateside. He was hale and hearty, no injuries to speak of. I assume he got at least one of the messages I sent telling him I was pregnant."

With a half-shrug, she added, "He never looked me up after he returned. Eventually he got stationed elsewhere and left the area. It's not as though my name has changed, and I made sure he had my parents' address before he left. He's had plenty of opportunity to find me in the years since, but as far as I know, he's never tried. At some point, I stopped wondering if I'd hear from him."

"I've read some of your articles. You're always supportive of those who serve in the armed forces. I guess I'm kind of surprised after hearing your story. It would have been easy for you to hold his actions against everyone who ever put on a uniform."

Avery shook her head. "Nah. If I buy a bag of oranges, and the first one I pull out is rotten, I'm not going to assume the whole bag needs to be tossed. It happened that the first man I got involved with was a rotten orange. His being in the military was coincidence. I'm pretty sure he would have been a rotten orange no matter what his career."

"On behalf of men everywhere, I apologize for the rotten orange."

"It's okay," she said with a half-smile. "I mean, don't get me wrong, I'm sure I'd kick him as hard as I could if I saw him now, but not because of me."

"Because of Eli," Gavin guessed.

She nodded.

"Hard as it may be to swallow, Eli might be better off without him. I mean, if this is the kind of man he is, then what kind of influence would he be on your son?"

"I know," she said, "but every child should know they're loved. Every child should feel valued. No child should have to grow up knowing one of their parents didn't want them."

Her hands were clenched in her lap, and Gavin reached over and rested one of his hands on hers. "I think you've covered all those bases. You can't force the man to be a part of Eli's life, but that kid will never doubt your love. He has grown up knowing what it means to be wanted and valued. There are lots of kids out there with two parents who can't say the same thing."

Avery pulled one of her hands out of his grasp and rested it on top of his. With his hand sandwiched between both hers, he felt every nuance of her touch, and warmth moved through him, starting at the fingertips and moving its way to his chest.

****

They drove along in peaceful quiet with nothing but the soft sound of the radio in the background for the next several miles. Avery had shared more with Gavin than she had anybody else in a long time. First, asking him about Eli's faith, and then telling him about her son's father.

She didn't understand why, but she trusted him in a deep-down way that didn't feel as foreign to her as she thought it should. Surprised by her reaction to him, Avery finally acknowledged that she wanted to get to know him better, and not just in the usual surface way. A practical person at heart, facts usually shaped her logical approach to any situation. With Gavin, though, it was somehow different. The events of his life didn't matter as much as how they'd affected him, and logic was overruled by how she felt when she was around him.

"What about you? I imagine when you were ready to go back to work, you could have gotten a job anywhere. How'd you end up at the Albuquerque Times?"

Gavin let out a sardonic laugh. His hand, which he'd reclaimed for driving a few miles back, now tugged at his stocking cap.

"I burned a lot of bridges." He stopped, his hand tapping out a beat on the steering wheel. "When I decided to take care of my mom, I quit everything, walked away. People were left in the lurch because of my choices. As a result, a lot of them ended up with a sour taste in their mouths whenever my name came up. Plus, some other new up-and-coming stars were on the rise. Similar to any fame-based industry, once your name is forgotten for even a week, you can be replaced. And I was. Replaced, that is."

"I'm sure there were some people out there still willing to give you a chance."

He nodded, "There were, but I needed to figure out what I wanted to do with the rest of my life. I wasn't sure I wanted to head back into the world I'd been in before. While I went into photojournalism because I wanted to make a difference, the reality of the industry is a lot more political than I'd realized when I made that choice. I wasn't sure I wanted to go back." He stopped long enough to adjust the air vents for the heater and to give the rearview mirror the tiniest shift to the left. "Spending those last years with Mom reminded me of the simpler times when life had a slower pace and everyone was happier."

"Slow isn't always bad," she said.

He chuckled. "No, I think it's pretty good. When Audrey asked me if I'd be interested in doing some work for Mitchell, I balked. The idea of a pity job didn't appeal. She was my sister, and I loved her for it, but I didn't want her forcing her husband to give me a job. Then Mitchell called a couple days later to say it had been his idea, not Audrey's. He'd asked her to call because he thought she'd be better at convincing me. I might not have been able to find the kind of work I wanted, but my name still garnered enough recognition that he thought it would bring some credibility to the Times."

"It did. It's your name and skill as a photographer that brought our small town feature to national attention and got us syndication."

"Don't say so during contract negotiations, or you'll get burned," he said with a quiet laugh trilling through his words like a clarinet in concert.

"Do you enjoy working for the Times?" She was fishing for information but hoped he wouldn't catch on.

The smile on his face said he had a pretty good idea what she was digging for.

"The syndication forced me to sign papers, so I've committed the next year to Mitchell. I figure I owed him at least that much. He's been good to me, both personally and professionally. There are a lot of snakes out there, and he's not one of them. I can live with giving him the next year of my life."

Another minute later, Avery said, "I hate to say anything, but…"

Gavin finished the sentence, "…the heat's gone out."

# Chapter Thirteen

Hollis, OK
December 24, 7:15 p.m.

"There's one!" Avery pointed to a looming sign for a truck stop, and Gavin navigated the car in the correct direction. As it came to a stop in one of the parking spots, she asked, "Are you sure they'll be able to help with the heat?"

Gavin shrugged and said, "If not, they can tell us who might be able to. We won't make it without heat. The windows are fogging up too bad, and with the passenger window taped closed, I can't ask you to roll it down and help me to see. Besides, if nothing else, they'll have a windshield wiper for us."

"Or a portable defroster," Eli said.

Avery spun to her son and asked, "A what?"

He gave her a smug look and said, "I know more than you think I do about the *real world*. They sell portable defrosters that plug into the cigarette lighter. I don't know how effective they are, but I know they're out there."

The always-in-control parent in her wanted to ask him

how he knew about things like that, but, in all honesty, what did it matter? *It's not as if he claimed to know how to roll a joint. Knowing about DC-powered defrosters isn't exactly a red flag of pending parental doom.*

They entered the truck stop together. Avery headed straight for the restroom. *One of these days I'll go see a doctor… Oh, who am I kidding? One of these days I won't make it in time, and then I'll be motivated to go see someone for a prescription. I don't remember learning about these kinds of consequences in sex ed.*

As she'd come to expect from him, by the time she'd exited the restroom, Gavin had found the replacement windshield wiper and was juggling two different defrosters that could plug into the cigarette lighter. He was comparing information on the box.

When she approached, he said, "I'm thinking we should get both." As he continued to scrutinize the boxes, he added, "In case one works better than the other."

"How does it work?" She wanted to know.

He showed her the picture. "Plug it in, and then place it on the dashboard directed toward the window you need cleared."

A burly trucker, well over six feet tall, with a big bushy beard, stopped by them and said, "You got defroster trouble?" His hulking presence made the narrow aisle shrink around them. Noticing for the first time that they were in a dead-end aisle, Avery tried to inch her way toward freedom only to realize there was no way to get past the trucker without first asking him to move.

Gavin, who Avery had thought of as tall, needed to look up at this man. "Uh, yeah," he said, craning his neck. "The heat went out, and we need to make it to Nowhere."

"Nowhere?" Puzzled, the trucker said, "You ain't gonna find nothing in Nowhere. Passed through there not too long ago. Place is shut down tight. Gone for the holidays, I'd say."

Looking at Gavin, Avery tried to silently communicate

her disbelief. *He's got to be thinking of a different town.*

"What you drivin'?" the behemoth of a man asked.

Nodding toward their barely visible car, Gavin said, "Older-model, small hatchback."

"And you've been able to drive okay on these roads? In that little thing?"

"We've managed."

Eli, who had again snuck near without notice, declared from the other side of the trucker, "We had a flat tire, and the spare wasn't aired up. Right after that, the bumper fell off. Then the thermostat stopped working and the car kept overheating. The windshield wipers fell off. Um... what else? Oh yeah. The passenger window got stuck down. Then the heat went out." He craned his neck until he caught view of his mom around the side of the trucker's arm and asked, "Did I miss anything?"

Embarrassment scorched through Avery, making her heart thump out a *ground-please-swallow-me-now* beat. The poor trucker gawked at them before running a giant hand over his hairy face. He swallowed a couple times, which Avery could see from her vantage point under his Adam's apple. There was hair growing on it. She'd never noticed before that a man's beard could grow down so low on his neck. *I'll bet that's a difficult spot to shave.*

Eventually the trucker asked, "And why exactly are y'all still traveling?"

"Long story," Gavin said. "Do you have any suggestions about a portable defroster, or where we can go to get our defroster fixed?"

The trucker looked at them suspiciously. Then he blinked a couple times and shook his head, his beard keeping beat with the movement. It seemed like he'd given up on expecting them to be reasonable.

Touching one of the boxes, the trucker said, "This one should do the trick for you. It's the better of the two. With all the trouble you've been having, though, you might want to get two. And one of these cans to fix a flat tire. Maybe some oil, too. He started retracing his steps out of the close-ended automotive aisle, handing them more items with each step. By the time he was done, they had everything from flashlights and shiny metallic emergency blankets to duct tape and flares. Lots of flares.

The mammoth man led them up to the cash register then stepped outside to take a look at their car. When he came back in, he shook his head and said, "You're crazy to be going to Nowhere, Oklahoma, this time of year, let alone this time of night."

"We have our orders," Gavin said. "Besides, we've come too far to turn back now. And it hasn't been all bad. I've gotten to know two complete strangers here." He waved his hand toward Avery and Eli.

Studying the group before him, the trucker swiveled his head back and forth between each of them. "You mean you aren't a family?"

Avery pulled Eli close and said, "We're family, and by the time this trip is over and that rental car is returned, I'm pretty sure we'll have adopted him, too." She waved toward Gavin as she said those last words.

Then the trucker again stared over to where the car was parked. "A rental?"

They all nodded.

"Y'all got ripped, you know that, right?"

Avery's mouth felt dry. She could hear her heart pounding in her ears. Eli had to say, "Mom, let go," to get her to realize how tightly she'd been squeezing his arm.

It wasn't the trucker's fault they'd gotten such a horrible car. *Yeah, but he didn't have to point it out, either.*

"We appreciate your help," Gavin said, indicating the defrosters and the pile of safety gear the man had heaped on them. The cashier was ringing it up but didn't have a big

119

enough bag to put it all in. "It's okay," Gavin said to her. "Bag it however you can. We'll be fine."

The trucker didn't say much after that, but he waved them off as they pulled out of their parking spot and headed toward the gas pumps.

****

After Gavin gassed up the car, Avery offered to drive.

"No, that's okay. I've still got plenty of juice in me." He was willing to say almost anything to keep her out of the driver's seat.

"I may have gotten pulled over in Amarillo, but that doesn't mean I'm a bad driver. You're safe with me behind the wheel."

"It's not that. I make a better driver than passenger," he said, hoping she would let the subject drop.

"This is because I was driving when the thermostat died."

"No, it's not. Honest." *Come on. Give it up and get into the passenger seat.*

Hands on her hips, eyes squinted, Avery said, "Then it's because I was driving when the windshield wipers came off."

Gavin shook his head and moved to the passenger side of the car. "Have it your way, Avery. Go ahead. Get in."

*Just tell her already.*

He ignored his inner voice and watched as Avery settled into the driver's seat. The seat was reclining so far back, she was more or less looking straight up. Never mind reaching the pedals, they were way beyond where her toes could stretch.

Avery pulled herself out of the car and began running her hands under the edge of the seat and along the back. Once she found it, she yanked downward on an adjustment lever, but nothing happened. She tried again, this time tugging at the seat-back with her other hand. "Push it forward, Eli," she instructed.

Eli pushed, grunting with the effort, but the seat-back refused to be moved.

Squatting on the cold cement next to the car, which was still parked by the gas pump, Avery eyed Gavin, who was now sitting in the passenger seat, and said, "It appears to be stuck."

He nodded.

"You knew it was stuck."

He again moved his head in the affirmative.

"Were you at any point going to tell me about this?"

"Not so much, no. I thought I'd keep driving, and you wouldn't need to know."

Avery shook her head and returned to the passenger side of the hatchback. "I suppose you can drive then."

Gavin happily climbed out of the seat he'd been keeping warm and moved back to the other side of the car.

"When did it get stuck?" Avery, it seemed, wasn't going to let it go until she had all the information. No wonder she'd gone into journalism.

"Not a clue," he replied. "I first noticed it in Clarendon after I got the window up, but I don't know if that's when it started or not."

"Why didn't you want to tell me?"

Gavin gave an exasperated shrug and answered, "It seems silly now, but so many things have gone wrong. I didn't want to add another one to the list."

Avery smiled at him and said. "You're right. It is silly. But thoughtful. In a weird, trying-to-protect-the-damsel kind of way."

Watching the road, Gavin still couldn't help but smile. So, in Avery's world, rescuing a damsel was considered weird. That bit of information might prove useful someday.

He'd watched her in the truck stop and had taken note of the way she'd handled herself. When the trucker first approached them, she'd been scared. She'd blinked rapidly and backed up when the large man had come close. By the time the trucker got around to saying something about her family, she'd gotten over her fear and had passed straight on through to defensive. As soon as the words about them not being family had left the trucker's mouth, her chin had gone up, and her eyes had dared the giant of a man to disagree with anything she'd said.

*Adopted.*

What would it be like to get adopted by Avery and Eli? To be a part of their lives on a regular basis? To spend time with them that wasn't in a car they'd all been forced into?

"Do you ever wonder how different this trip might have gone if you'd gotten the original SUV you were supposed to get?"

His question hung in the air between them for a little while before she answered. "Having seen the rental lot, I'm not sure it would have turned out much differently than it has, except repairs would be more expensive, I suppose."

"That's not what I mean."

She shrugged. "You mean, if we were all comfy and in a vehicle big enough where we could each have an entire bench seat to ourselves?"

"Yeah, something along that line."

"I don't know," she said. "You thought I was a man, and you were pretty determined to dislike me for being a woman. Would you have been able to get over it?"

He laughed. "Talking is one of the things I do best. I would have tried to engage you in conversation to get to know you better. Or, if I foolishly still didn't care for you because you're a woman, I would have tried to talk to Eli."

"You're good at that."

His heart warmed at the compliment. "My mom taught me years ago to look behind the person to the story."

"I'm a journalist. I look for the story."

He shook his head. "It's not the same. Journalists tend to look for the story, but they often miss the people. Photographers can get so preoccupied with the people that they miss the story."

"But a good photojournalist," said Avery, "sees both."

"I have talked to people all over the world. Everyone," he said, nodding for emphasis, "has a story. They may not all want to share it, but everyone has one. You show a little genuine interest in that story, and most people will open up to you and bend over backward to lend you a hand if you need it."

As he glanced over at her, he could see the wheels turning in Avery's head.

"You disagree?" he asked.

"No, not so much. I think 'genuine' is the key word. It's not something you can fake. If you try to engage someone in conversation because you want to get something out of them, it won't get you anywhere."

"Whether they recognize it or not, most people instinctively know when they're being played," he said. "Try to schmooze someone because you want something, and you're no better than a used car salesman. People know that."

"Shmooze?" Eli piped up to ask, "What, is this an eighties' movie now, or something?"

"How do you know that word's from the eighties?" Avery asked.

"Well, it's definitely not from this century, and I don't think even the nineties would have wanted it, so…"

After another couple minutes, Gavin asked, "So, Eli, do you think we'd all be getting along this well if we'd had a nice big comfortable vehicle to drive in?"

The teen leaned forward as far as his seatbelt would allow and got his head up close to his mom's ear before saying, "Mom's a tough nut to crack, so I don't know. I've been telling her forever now that she needs to start dating again. The way I see it, all this close togetherness with someone of the opposite sex is good practice for her. It'll help her get back into shape so she doesn't embarrass herself when I do finally convince her to accept a date with a real live man."

Gavin kept his eyes smartly locked onto the pavement in front of him. Avery, yet again a victim to Eli's perfect timing, was choking on her water. Eli sat back in his seat, popped his earbuds into place, and winked at Gavin in the rearview mirror.

A smile started to stretch across Gavin's mouth, but he schooled his features as soon as Avery looked his way. He didn't think she was ready yet to know how much he agreed with young Eli.

# Chapter Fourteen

Altus, OK
December 24, 8:00 p.m.

"Altus looks like a nice town," Avery said as they drove through. "It might be interesting to visit here sometime. In the daylight. When it's not the middle of winter."

Gavin let her make conversation. It wasn't something she volunteered to do often. In fact, up to that point, he'd noticed she'd primarily gotten talkative when she was embarrassed or uncomfortable.

"We are passing straight on through," he said. "We've got about another ninety minutes, two hours tops, before we get to Nowhere."

"I haven't seen any signs for it. Have you?"

He shook his head. "Must not be big enough to warrant listing on a highway sign."

"I want to get to Nowhere, get a hotel room, fall into a big soft comfy bed, and order room service."

"On Mitchell's dime, of course," he said. "Or at Corporate's expense, actually. I hope they're the ones who end up footing the bill."

Avery twisted around to better see him, "Have you heard back from him? Did he reply to any of your texts?"

Gavin shook his head. "I lost cell service again and haven't regained it. If he's texted me, I haven't gotten them yet. Have you heard from him?"

Realizing her phone had been unusually silent, Avery took it out and frowned. "Dead battery. I forgot to charge it when we stopped at the hotel earlier."

"What about you, Eli?" Gavin asked. "Any cell service?"

Eli gazed blankly at his phone then shrugged. "I charged my MP3 player at the hotel but forgot to charge my phone. I've got the DC-powered charger for it, and the same one fits Mom's phone."

"Yeah," Avery said, "but with our portable defroster plugged in there, we can't charge the phone."

"Oh well," Gavin said. "It won't hurt him too much to stew. We'll call him as soon as we get there."

Altus was in their rearview mirror by the time Eli said, "Hey guys, do you think we can stop? I could use a restroom."

Exasperated, Avery circled toward him and said, "We *just* passed through a town. Why didn't you say anything then?"

"I didn't have to go then."

Two minutes passed.

"I *really* need to go. Pull over, and I'll find a bush."

Gavin chuckled at the mortified look on Avery's face. If it weren't for his presence, he was pretty sure the teen would be getting a lecture on timing. For the dozenth time. Then again, Gavin had to wonder if his very presence was part of what was motivating Eli to push the limits with his mom.

As the car came to a stop, Eli bolted from his seat, flashlight in hand.

"I'm so sorry," Avery said.

"No problem," he replied. "We all have to go sometime.

All in all, Eli's been a great traveling companion. I haven't heard him complain. Despite everything that's happened. And he hasn't once asked if we're there yet, which makes him tops in my book."

After a couple heartbeats, he heard Avery mutter, "Great."

Gavin peered at her. "What's the problem?"

With a deep inhale and exhale, she said, "Now I have to go."

By the time Avery fished the toilet paper out from its hiding spot in the back seat, Eli had returned.

It was dark out but not quite pitch-black yet. "Come on," Gavin said to Eli. "Let's go take a look at the other side of the road."

"Why?" the teen asked, looking puzzled as he pushed his hands deeper into his jacket's pockets.

"Come with me, and don't argue about it."

"Okay," Eli said, "but mostly because Mom is frantically waving me in your direction."

When they got to the opposite side of the road, Gavin told him, "Your mom needs to go, too, but there's not much in the way of shrubs or trees on this stretch of the road. So you and I will enjoy the scenery over here until your mom's ready for us to go back over there," he said, pointing in the general direction of the hatchback.

"Huh." Looking around, Eli said, "I never would have thought of that."

Gavin shrugged, "Someday you'll reach the point where, no matter what you're doing, you'll wonder if it's going to work for a girl or how one would feel about it."

"You should ask her out on a date when we get back to Albuquerque, you know."

He took a quick peek at Eli but couldn't make out much more than the shadow of his face in the early winter night. "Why do you think so?"

Eli held out a hand and began ticking off fingers. "You laugh at her corny jokes. You don't ignore me. You handle stress pretty well." Then he paused and said, "Trust me, there's a lot of stress where my mom's concerned. Especially if she doesn't get her coffee." Going back to his fingers, he said, "You understand her work. Her voice gets all fuzzy when she talks to you."

Gavin adjusted his scarf and said, "I'll take it under advisement." The boy's words made him feel as if he could take on the world, and he was pretty sure he wasn't doing a good job of hiding that fact from Eli.

"Besides," the younger man added, "I'm going to leave for college someday. Who knows where I'll go or what I'll do after that."

"I understand," Gavin replied.

"Maybe you do, maybe you don't," Eli said cryptically. "The thing is, I don't want her to be alone. She needs someone in her life. She won't admit it, and maybe she doesn't even realize it, but it's true."

He heard Avery's call from across the road and wheeled around, a feeling of lightness in his chest and limbs. *Huh. Dating advice from Eli. And I think I like it.*

The two of them took their first step onto the road when a car came out of nowhere, followed by the screaming sound of metal tearing against metal.

Gavin instinctively reached out his arm and threw Eli behind him until the sound stopped. A quick look told him the boy was fine. Then he took off running across the road. "Avery!"

He found her in the snow on the other side of the car. She was dazed but didn't appear hurt. "Are you okay? Did you get hit?"

She shook her head then winced. "I saw the headlights a second before it hit. I jumped back to avoid it, but I tripped and fell. I think I hit my head."

Gavin pulled his hands out of his gloves and tenderly felt her head. He could tell where a knot was forming, but the area didn't feel wet or sticky. "I think you got a good bump, but it doesn't appear to have broken any skin. It might be a good idea to see a doctor to make sure you didn't get a concussion."

Eli joined them then. "Everyone okay?"

"I'm fine," Avery said, pushing to her feet. "Did the driver stop?"

"He's long gone," the teen said, shaking his head.

"We were all the way over in the emergency lane, weren't we?" Avery asked.

Nodding, Eli said, "I took another look. We're off the road, but with the snow everywhere and this fog descending, the driver might not have noticed the white car sitting there. I'll bet he'd have seen the Zeon."

Avery rolled her eyes then winced again. "You're never going to let it go, are you?"

"Not on your life," the boy said as though nothing was wrong.

Gavin peeked at Eli, wondering why the boy wasn't asking how his mom was doing. That's when he saw it. Eli was white as a sheet, and his hands were trembling. He was masking it in his voice, but the kid was undeniably worried about his mom.

"Eli, stay here with your mom. She got a bump on the head, but she's fine. I'm going to take a look at the car." Then he gently pushed Avery back down into a sitting position and whispered in her ear, "He needs to know you're okay."

Stepping away, he went to the car and circled around it a couple times. He let out a low whistle and said, "We should report this to the highway patrol, but since none of us have working phones…"

"Is it drivable?" Avery asked. "We can't stay out here on the side of the road through the night."

Eli said, "Maybe if we lit a bunch of those roadside flares, someone would stop to help us."

Gavin tried to open the driver's side door, but it wouldn't budge. He climbed in through the passenger side and settled into the driver's seat, worried that the car might not start. When the engine engaged without a problem, he left it idling and climbed back out.

"The car's pretty scraped up on the driver's side, and that door won't even open. The engine sounds a little rough, too, but it's running, so I say let's pile back into it and get as far away from here as we can.

Eli and Avery stood, with the teen putting his arm around his mom's shoulders to help guide her to the car. "I'm not an invalid, you know. It's nothing but a bump on the head."

Gavin could hear the teen's words as he answered back, "Humor me."

Once they were all settled into the car and belted in place, Gavin checked his mirrors and pulled out onto the road. "I can't believe I never saw it coming. I'm still not even sure what kind of car it was. There's no way I'll be able to identity it when we're able to file a report."

"It was blue," Eli said.

"No," Avery countered. "Green."

Gavin thought it had been black but couldn't stop himself from having a little fun. "I was going to say yellow."

They'd made it less than half a mile down the road when Avery said, "You should get up to the speed limit so no one comes up too fast on our rear bumper."

"We don't have a rear bumper, so no problem there!" Eli's voice was far too cheerful.

*What kind of fool idea was it to raise this boy to find the humor in troubled times?*

Frowning, Gavin said, "I think the sideswipe did more damage than I'd realized." As he accelerated, the car began to vibrate more and more.

"Did you check the tires? Maybe we have a flat?" Eli asked.

Gavin shook his head, "I checked the tires. They're all fine. I think we've lost a cylinder."

"How do you lose a cylinder?" Avery asked with skepticism. "Should we go back for it?"

"Not literally," he replied. "I think one of the cylinders is damaged. Something happened so it's not working properly."

"And you know this how?" came from Avery.

"It happened to a car my mom had once," he replied.

"Did her car get hit, too?" Eli asked.

Shaking his head, Gavin said, "No. Something inside the engine got loose and damaged it. I'm not sure if the sideswipe could have done this or if this is a problem that might have already been building up, and the sideswipe just knocked something around to finalize the problem."

"Does it even matter what caused it at this point?" Avery asked.

Gavin sighed, bringing the car back down to a slower speed with less vibrating. Thirty-five miles per hour was going to make the last two hours of the drive stretch out into more than four. "Probably not," he answered, "but I was trying to decide if I should add this to my mental list of grievances against the car. It doesn't seem fair at this point to have a problem we *can't* blame on the car."

Avery shook her head and said, "This might go down in the record books as the worst Christmas trip ever."

"It's all about perspective," Eli said. "I'm kind of having fun wondering what's going to go wrong next. Although I could have done without the last one."

Gavin studied Avery for a moment before asking, "Are you doing okay?"

She nodded gingerly and said, "I'm fine. I'm pretty certain there's no concussion. I don't have any blurred vision or muddled thinking. At least not that I can tell," she added with a smirk. "A good-sized headache for sure, but that's all."

Thinking he might have to force the issue when they got somewhere with an urgent care center or emergency room, Gavin let it go.

"On the bright side," he said instead, "the car that hit us must have done some good, too. The headlights are now a lot brighter."

Avery chuckled softly. "Now we can better see how we're in the middle of nowhere. Yay."

"Nah," Eli said. "We're not in the middle yet. We haven't even reached the city limits. This must be the outskirts of Nowhere."

# Chapter Fifteen

Hobart, OK
December 24, 9:30 p.m.

By the time they passed through Hobart, everyone in town appeared to be fast asleep. Avery imagined all the little kids tucked into their beds and waiting for Christmas morning. "This is a quaint little town."

"And then it was gone," Gavin said.

Sure enough, the town of Hobart had passed them by before he'd even finished his sentence.

"The sign when we entered said the population was less than four thousand," Gavin added.

"But did you see that main street? It reminded me of a small town my grandma used to live in when she was alive."

With a mock groan, he said, "You're going to want to take this trip again someday, aren't you?"

Avery beamed and said, "On a weekend. In my own car. During the summer."

Gavin shook his head and said, "You're a glutton, that's for sure."

"I can't help it. I'm naturally curious."

"Let me guess," he said. "You want to know if the events of this trip can be duplicated."

She reached forward toward the dashboard and stretched. Her shoulders were starting to tighten up, no doubt from the fall she'd taken at their last stop. "Admit it," she eventually said. "If we take another trip on this road, and it ends up as dismal as this one has been, I'll be able to write a whole series of articles on the worst road ever traveled."

"Even if the circumstances never duplicate, I think you've still got enough material for at least a couple articles about travel disasters. You could spin them so they're about travel preparedness, the things people should plan for ahead of time."

"Like we did?" she asked.

Gavin glanced over, and she saw the humor lighting his coffee brown eyes from within. Her breath caught in her chest as she drank in what she saw there. His gaze returned to the road far too quickly. She savored the memory of that look and how it made her feel. It had been a long time since she'd let someone get close enough to look at her in that way… and for it to have an effect on her.

She turned to face the dark road ahead and reached over to turn on the radio. Surfing through the channels, she searched for one playing a familiar song. Once she settled on a station, she snuggled into the passenger seat and pulled her jacket in around her. Avery needed some time to think.

*The last time I had this strong a reaction to a guy, I ended up pregnant.* Gavin wasn't so much a guy as he was a man, a far cry from… *And I'm not a girl anymore, either. This is different.*

In the years since college, Avery hadn't dated anyone seriously. In fact, she'd hardly dated at all. Her role as Mom had taken precedence over everything else. With a child to provide for, she'd worked hard. Between Eli and her job, all her time had been consumed. Her energy, too.

Letting someone get close enough to hurt her – or her son – had been the farthest thing from her mind. At first it was because of the way she'd been stung by Eli's father. Then it became a matter of survival. Single parenthood had been hard, and she'd poured everything she'd had into making sure her son had felt the lack of father as little as possible.

Gavin had been spot-on. Eli was good kid. Her job wasn't over, not by a long shot. Maybe, though, she'd finally reached a place where she could take a step back. *Am I ready to let someone into my life? Into our lives?*

Having been raised by a single mom, Gavin would understand the risks better than most. He would know the balance she wanted, the kind that would allow both her son and the man in her life to share the limelight. She wouldn't be willing to make Eli less important so the person she was dating could feel more important.

"I'm hungry." Eli's voice intruded into her thoughts.

Avery smiled to herself. *Face it. Eli would never allow himself to be made less important.*

"You've got the snack bag. Surely there's something good to eat in there. After all, you're the one who packed it."

Eli rummaged around in the back seat for a while. "Yeah, about that," he eventually said.

Any other day, Avery would have been put on the alert by Eli's voice. She would have felt the hair on the back of her neck rise as she waited for the other shoe of Eli's conversation to drop. Too many things, however, had gone wrong in the last day-and-a-half. There wasn't much Eli could say at present that would bother her.

"I might have forgotten the bag with snacks back at the hotel."

Avery swiveled in her seat to take a look at her son. "You might have?"

He blushed. "I sort of totally forgot it."

She threw her head back and laughed, which ended up

hurting more than she'd expected it to. Eli gawked at her as if she'd told him to dissect a live rodent that had gone swimming in toxic guano. She could see Gavin smirking as he continued driving at a snail's pace.

"Oh, Eli. I wish this trip had gone so smoothly that a misplaced bag of food could bother me. Alas, that isn't even annoying enough to be a blip on the disaster radar."

Eli grumbled.

"What was that?" Avery asked him.

"You might not think it's a disaster," he said, "but I'm still hungry."

She laughed some more and said, "Maybe we'll find an open gas station in the next town."

"Not likely," Gavin said. "It seems that every small town in Oklahoma shuts down at eight o'clock sharp on Christmas Eve."

"Okay," Eli said. "I was on the fence before, but this has now officially become the worst Christmas Eve *ever*."

*Everything else must pale in comparison to the loss of food.*

"I respect your priorities, Eli," Gavin said.

The words had barely left Gavin's mouth when his phone started chiming. He reached for it and took a quick look. "I must have a signal. A bunch of texts from Mitchell showed up, and all the ones that were in my outbox are now gone." Giving the phone a light toss in Avery's direction, he said, "See if you can call him."

She caught the phone and pulled Mitchell's name up from the contact list and pressed *call*. It rang one, twice... and then she got disconnected. She tried again. This time she got one ring before it disconnected. After shaking the phone, Avery again pressed the *call* button. No luck.

"We lost the signal," she said.

"Either you have the worst cell service ever, or a whole boatload of cell towers are down," said Eli.

Gavin sighed. "I think the car emits a field of energy

preventing communication. Think about it. The only times we've been able to call for help are when we've been out of the car."

Eli shook his head. "Everything seems to be going a lot more smoothly since the car got hit. Maybe the guy who sideswiped it did us a favor."

"All I have to do to change that," Gavin replied, "is press on the gas and bring this baby up higher than thirty miles per hour. Then your teeth will rattle right on out of your head."

"Okay, okay," Eli said. "You have to admit, though, aside from that, we've made it through, like, two whole towns, and without any problems. That's practically a record."

Avery's chin dropped to her chest as she shook her head. "Please tell me you did not just say that out loud."

Before anybody could utter a word, the car came to a jarring stop.

# Chapter Sixteen

Carnegie, OK
December 24, 10:50 p.m.

Gavin sat there. He gripped the steering wheel so tightly his knuckles were white and his hands began to ache. Dread swept through him as he realized that yet one more thing had gone wrong. Through gritted teeth, he managed to ask, "Is everyone okay?"

"What happened?" Avery asked as she pushed at the airbag that had come flying out at her from the dashboard.

"I'm never saying things are going good again, I promise," said Eli.

"Everyone's okay?" Gavin asked again, his jaw muscles beginning to relax.

"Yeah, we're fine," Avery said, watching him with her eyebrows drawn together, and questions lurking in her beautiful green eyes.

"I think the axel broke." His movements were abrupt as he batted away the deployed air bag. Resting at a drunken angle with the front driver side sunken low, the hatchback felt precariously balanced. Gavin scanned the area outside his window to make sure they were still on the road and not hanging over some heretofore unseen precipice. The way this trip had been going, finding a gaping ravine under his door seemed more likely than finding asphalt. As he searched with his eyes, he saw faded roadway dusted with remnants of the snowstorm.

Turning to Avery, Gavin said, "I need to get out and see what's wrong."

She gazed at him blankly for a minute before her eyes widened, and she shook her head. "Sorry. I forgot your door's not working. Hold on." She opened her door and got out so he could climb across the gearshift and follow suit.

By the time Gavin exited the car, Eli was out, too. "I'm not sure I want to stay in there alone anymore. Somehow it doesn't seem safe."

"Here's the problem," Avery called from the other side of the car.

Gavin sauntered around to where she stood near the front end on the driver's side. There was a hole in the road, easily two feet across, and he'd driven the front of the car into it.

Pulling the stocking cap from his head, Gavin said, "I swear it wasn't there a minute ago. I was watching the road. I would have noticed something as big as that."

Eli and his mother both squatted down to examine the hole.

"It's a puddle," the teen said.

Avery was fingering the jagged shards of ice at the edge of the hole. "I think it was frozen over. As dark as it is, and with snow blown across the frozen top, it's no wonder you didn't see it."

Gavin ran his fingers through his crisp black hair. "I'm at the end of my rope here. I'm half-tempted to kick the other tires, but I'm afraid if I do, they'll fall off, or worse, instantaneously combust."

Standing back up, Avery said, "I think the axel's okay. The car's small. If we work together, we might be able to lift it out of the hole."

"Once we do," Eli added, "we should light some flares to mark the area around it so nobody else falls in."

"I'm sorry, guys," Gavin said.

Head angled to the side, Avery gave him an odd look and said, "It's okay. We're fine. We can fix this."

"This entire trip has been nothing but one disaster after another." Gavin wasn't willing to let it go.

"It's not such a big deal," Eli said. "We're living in a B-rated movie, but a lot more original. I'm not going to have to go to the theater for months after we get back to Albuquerque because nothing those scriptwriters can come up with is going to be able to compare to real life."

They were trying to make him feel better, and he appreciated it. Still… "It's my job to make sure you guys get there safely, and I'm not doing a very good job of that."

Her brow furrowed again, Avery frowned and tugged on her scarf. "It was never your job to keep us safe."

Shaking his head, Gavin said, "See, I know that. It doesn't change the fact that I feel responsible for you both. But what happens? You almost got hit the last time we stopped!" With a booming voice, he yelled to the cast-over sky, "This is getting ridiculous!"

Avery's eyes moved furtively from him to Eli. Gavin knew what she was thinking. *I need to get my son away from the madman.*

Gavin scratched his head then tugged his stocking cap back on. "Okay. I feel better now. Let's see if we can lift this baby out of here."

He approached the car, and Avery took two steps back. Feeling back in control, he winked at her and said, "I needed to let off a little steam. I'm okay now. Honest."

She shook her head and said, "You had me worried."

"Nah," he said. "No need to worry about me. I'm as stable as they come. Why, I'm as rock-solid as this car." When her lips twitched, he asked, "Why is it that you haven't gotten angry yet? Aside from when you got pulled over back in Amarillo, I haven't seen you lose your cool once this whole trip."

"I heard this sermon once," Avery answered. "Did you know when God brought His people out of Egypt, He didn't take them in a straight path to get where they were going? He knew they wouldn't be able to handle what was on the straight path, so He took them a roundabout way to get there. When we got to the detour after Amarillo, it just kind of hit me. I think this is our roundabout way. It might not make sense to anyone but me, but the way I see it, God is still guiding our path, even though that path isn't going the direction we want it to go. I've still gotten frustrated and haven't exactly been singing His praises the whole way, but despite that, I just have this feeling inside that we're exactly where God wants us to be."

"For someone who doesn't feel comfortable talking about her faith, you did a fine job explaining that." Gavin watched as Avery became suddenly busy examining the far side of the car. He couldn't help but smile. He was sure that, if it weren't for the freezing air that had already turned all their cheeks a ruddy color, he'd have spotted a blush on her face. "Avery?" When she glanced up at him, he said, "That's a great insight. Thank you for sharing it with me."

Then, before she had a chance to say anything in return, he began circling the hatchback. He walked around it twice, using his flashlight to highlight the extent of the hole in the pavement. "Okay, guys. We're going to put the car in neutral, then we're going to lift the front end and push the car so it's back on the road."

"We'll still have to get past the hole," Eli said.

Gavin nodded. "I can reverse and drive around it, no problem. It'll be easier to get the front of the car back than it will be to try to move the whole car forward."

"It's going to be tricky lifting the front and going over the hole as we back it up. We've lost the ability to grip an entire section of the car because of the hole," added Avery.

"I'm listening if anybody has a better idea."

"I'm in," Eli said. "Tell me where to stand."

Avery agreed. "I don't see a better way. But let's all please be careful not to fall into the hole. With the water in there, I can't see how deep it is."

Gavin directed everyone to their positions. Eli was on the passenger side of the engine. Avery was in front of the car but close to where her son was positioned. Gavin was alone on the driver's side by his own design. He didn't want to risk Avery or Eli tumbling into the hole. Wanting to avoid a face-first plummet into both the asphalt and the pit, he eyed his position and hoped he'd chosen well.

"On three," he said. "One, two, three."

The car proved lighter than they'd expected. It lifted easily out of the hole, and they were able to move it back onto the pavement with no trouble. Then, as they'd planned, once it was back on solid ground, Eli opened the passenger door, and Avery dove into the car to put the brake on and get it back into park.

Eli looked around and asked, "Was it supposed to be that easy?"

Gavin threw his head back and laughed. "I think I finally found a reason to be thankful for the hatchback. There's no way we could have lifted a giant SUV out of there." The tension released from his muscles, and he clapped his hand on Eli's back. "So how about some flares?"

It took a few minutes to get the flares out, but they used four to mark the area of the hole. Without a way to call out on any of their cellphones, they couldn't notify the highway patrol. Their best bet was hoping someone saw the flares and was better able to report the problem.

With nothing else to do, they climbed back into the car and headed down the road again.

The car definitely had a new vibration to it.

"Do you feel that?" Avery asked.

Gavin nodded. "We may not have broken the axel, but I'm pretty sure it's bent. We're going to have to limp along, but we should be able to manage. Nowhere shouldn't be much more than ten miles." He nodded confidently. "As long as we can get there, we'll be fine."

# Chapter Seventeen

Nowhere, Oklahoma
December 24, 11:40 p.m.

"We're almost there," Gavin said.

Avery, glad to hear the words, leaned forward in her seat, eager for her first look at Nowhere, Oklahoma. She had come to think of Nowhere as an oasis, a safe haven in the midst of all the troubles they'd had to deal with since leaving Albuquerque.

The hatchback struggled to climb a hill. Then Gavin, who couldn't accelerate the car over thirty because of the cylinder, held the clutch in and let the car glide down the other side. Without employing the use of the gas pedal, they were able to pick up some good speed that would give them momentum going into the next hill.

Avery watched the speedometer. Thirty. Forty. Fifty. Fifty-five.

A sound, like a tire popping, reached Avery's ears seconds before the most atrocious odor she'd ever smelled filled the car.

"What!" came Eli's choked voice from the back seat before he started gagging.

Gavin frantically pushed the button to roll his window down. He stuck his head out and started sucking in fresh air. Avery couldn't do the same. Her window was taped closed against the relief of fresh cold air.

Tears poured down her cheeks. Her vision was so obscured she almost didn't see the sign announcing they'd reached Nowhere, Oklahoma. *That can't be right.* She had to have seen it wrong. The sign listed the population as three. *Three!*

The first building they saw was a general store of sorts. Gavin deftly maneuvered the car into the vacant dirt parking lot, and they all three tumbled from the its interior.

Eli ran for some shrubs at the edge of the parking lot and doubled over, heaving.

Avery, collapsed onto all fours and started crawling away from the car.

When she took a glimpse back, Gavin was yanking everything out of the trunk. She knew she should help him, but her need for escape compelled her toward the store.

She'd made it about halfway to the steps of the general store before giving up. Sitting cross-legged, she watched as Gavin did what he could to rescue their belongings. Tears continued to course down her cheeks, and there was nothing she could do to stop them. The up-close-and-personal stink of the skunk was worse than anything she'd smelled in her life. Eli left the shrubs and joined her in the middle of the parking lot as the stench surrounding them battered the optimism and fighting spirit that had carried her along thus far on their journey.

Gavin, his muscles straining, carried both his camera cases and her suitcase to the front porch of the store. Then he carried his backpack, Eli's suitcase, and the emergency gear the trucker had insisted they purchase. Once he set it down on the front porch, he came back to where she and Eli sat in the dirt.

He held out a hand to Eli and said, "Come on. Let's go sit on the steps over there and figure this thing out."

Eli took the hand up and ambled toward the steps. When he got close, he spun back to them and made a face. Then he walked in a different direction and sat in the lone rusty chair left out in the parking lot toward the far end of the porch. It had probably been sitting there so the dump truck could collect it.

Gavin turned his eyes to Avery where she still sat in the dirt. He held out his hand and said, "Your turn. Let's get you as far away from the smell as we can."

"Don't bother! The luggage stinks to high heaven!" Eli's words weren't reassuring.

Once Avery gained her feet, she asked, "What happened?"

Gavin sighed, and his voice came in a monotone as he said, "I think we hit a skunk."

Avery was tired, hungry, and beyond the limits of what she felt she could endure. A bubble of hysteria rose in her chest. Before she knew it, she was laughing. It was a full-fledged belly laugh. She slapped her hand over her mouth and tried to contain it. When she heard Eli and Gavin joining her, she gave up and let the laughter win.

She soon found herself gasping for air as the edge of her vision began to darken. Reaching out, she grabbed Gavin's arm and felt her steps falter. There was nothing she could do to stop herself as she crashed into his side.

"Avery?"

Her head cleared, and she heard the concern in Gavin's voice. His arms were around her, holding her close. When her vision came into focus, she saw a pained look in his eyes, eyes that appeared even darker than usual because of how pale his face had become. She tried to say something, but her tongue felt thick within her mouth and wouldn't obey her commands.

"Avery?" he asked again, his jaw working against the words, his grip on her tightening.

She managed a shaky nod and said, "I'm okay."

"What was that? What happened?"

The tingle of heated embarrassment climbed her neck and passed over her face. Avery broke eye contact and shrugged. "Sometimes when I get carried away with laughter, I pass out."

"Are you sure that's all it was?"

Gavin's voice was tender. Avery was used to people cracking jokes or trying to make her laugh again when they learned her secret. Cruelty endured as a child had taught her to carefully guard her weakness from others. His reaction, the sound of his voice, the way he held her... it was different.

She could feel herself relaxing into his arms, her body shaping itself against his of its own accord. It had been a long time since a man had held her in anything other than a fatherly embrace. Her gaze skittered across his face, and her breath got stuck in her chest. His eyes were dark obsidian, but it wasn't worry she saw in them this time. It was...

Gavin lifted a hand to cup Avery's chin and bring her eyes back to meet his. His voice was a deep rumble as he asked, "Are you sure you're okay?"

She nodded, the motion sharp with uncertainty and the press of long-dormant emotions forcing their way to the surface of her consciousness.

He leaned in, and she closed her eyes. His lips rested against her forehead for the briefest moment, yet her skin felt branded by the touch.

Gavin let go, releasing her from his hold. Avery, however, continued to feel the warm touch of his arms around her, his lips on her skin. *It was a kiss on the forehead, you ninny! That's how Grandpa used to kiss you. It didn't mean anything!*

"Hey," Eli's voice called from where he sat. "It's

Christmas! You might as well get your cameras out and take some pictures, right, Gavin?"

"Christmas?" Avery asked. "It can't be."

Eli held up his phone and said, "It's a quarter after twelve. That makes it Christmas."

Avery trudged over to the front steps of the general store. She glowered at a notice on the door before sitting down. "It's Christmas. We're stuck here in a town that's been abandoned. We have nowhere to sleep, no way to exchange gifts, and we don't even have a Bible with us so we can read from Luke."

"What makes you say it's abandoned?" Gavin asked. "Maybe the people are sleeping." He nodded his head over toward a mobile home that sat on the other side of the general store, its windows black as the night sky.

"The sign on the door says they're closed till after the new year," Avery answered. "My guess is they're visiting family elsewhere. Looks like that trucker back in Hollis was right."

Gavin sat down next to her on the steps. Eli got up and moved his chair closer but managed to keep himself upwind of the luggage, which smelled putrid.

"I'll bet all our clothes are ruined," Avery offered. "I don't know if I can get back in that car. The smell is so awful."

Eli held up his phone and said, "I've got the Bible on here, Mom. Do you want me to read the chapter?"

It was their family tradition. She and Eli always started Christmas morning with the second chapter of Luke. Avery would have preferred to say she'd instituted the tradition because she was some sort of super-Christian who always knew what to do and say, and who had been raising her son to be a mighty evangelist since he'd been in diapers. In truth, she'd seen it on a cartoon and had liked the idea. That was when Eli was four. They'd been doing it ever since. Over the years it had become more meaningful to her, and to Eli, too, she hoped. She cast a quick glance at Gavin, wondering what he would think if he knew their Christmas morning tradition had been inspired by a cartoon. Would he laugh with them, or would he judge? *I don't think he has a judgmental bone in his body. He's almost too good to be true.*

Reining her wandering sleepy thoughts in, Avery asked, "Bible on your phone? Why didn't I know about that?"

Eli shrugged, "I always forget my Bible, but I never forget my phone. It's what I use at church, too."

"You mean... All those times I thought you were texting during church you were reading your Bible?"

Eli ducked his head before answering. "Maybe not all of them, but usually."

Avery gaped at her son a moment. Gavin had been right when he'd told her not to jump to conclusions about her son's faith. Then, raising her brow in confusion, she said, "I thought your phone was dead."

That's when she saw it. Eli hadn't moved any closer to them because he was tethered by an electrical cord. He'd found a place to plug in his phone! She needed to get hers plugged in, too, and see if they could call for help. First, though, she wanted to hear her son read. Giving him a nod, she closed her eyes and waited for him to begin.

"And it came to pass in those days that a decree went out from Caesar Augustus..."

Avery sighed, content with the journey. They might be in the middle of Nowhere, Oklahoma, in below freezing temperatures. They may even have endured the most horribly eventful journey in the history of road trips, but they were together, and aside from the stench clinging to each of them, they were well. It was Christmas, and her son had volunteered to read the Christmas story from the Bible he had stored on his phone. She peeked at Gavin and saw him listening with rapt attention as her son's words told of the Savior's birth. *I might be better off for having gotten stranded in the middle of Nowhere.*

She scooted closer to Gavin and leaned her head against

his shoulder. Sighing with contentment, she listened to Eli.

"...but Mary kept all these things and pondered them in her heart..."

When it was all said and done, Avery had a lot to be thankful for. She hadn't given much thought to the past in a long time. Gavin asking about Eli's father had brought up some of those memories, and for today, that was a good thing.

Remembering, she thought back to when she'd struggled working two jobs, trying to provide for Eli. She'd hated that he'd spent more time in daycare than with her. Each step of the way, however, God had put people into her path and Eli's life who had helped guide and love him, and that had supported and encouraged her. Without God's help and guidance, she never would have gotten where she was. She owned a home. It was old and small, but it was theirs. Eli was doing well and finding his own way. Her job was secure, and she felt valued in her work. Life wasn't perfect, but she was blessed.

"...And Jesus increased in wisdom and stature, and in favor with God and men."

"That was great, Eli. Thank you for reading it." Gavin's voice rumbled next to her ear.

Avery took a moment to say something in her heart to the God who sent His son to earth all those centuries ago and who, in all the years since, hadn't given up caring for His people. *First, I whined because we didn't have a Bible. Then I let my mind wander through the entire Christmas story. I am certainly not a super-Christian. Thank You for loving me anyway and for seeing us all through the things we've had to deal with in life. I might not be a rock star of the faith, but my faith in You is rock solid.* Wincing, she added, *Sorry for the bad pun. It was an accident.*

She sat up straight, pulled away from Gavin, and said to her son, "So, Eli, do you think we can make a call out on that phone you've got there? You know, since you have power now and all?"

As Eli nodded and began tapping the screen of his phone, a police cruiser pulled into the dirt parking lot.

Gavin jumped up from his seat but didn't move toward the newcomer. The officer climbed out and, from a distance, inspected their sad little white hatchback with the scraped-up and banged-in driver's side, the plastic passenger window, and all the doors and trunk flung open with the unmistakable smell of skunk rolling off it in waves. Then he studied the three forlorn people stranded in Nowhere and asked, "Where you folks from?"

"Albuquerque," Gavin answered. "We were sent to Nowhere to do a story for a newspaper, but it appears the higher-ups who ordered the story didn't realize there wasn't much here."

The officer had his headlights directed at them so he could see them clearly. He, however, was at best a fuzzy apparition to them. As he stepped closer, he blocked some of the light from his car and said, "I'm under orders to find y'all and deliver you down the road to Lawton. Seems as if you got some folks mighty worried about you."

"Who sent you to find us?" Gavin asked.

"Uh, well," the officer said. "Who *didn't* send me? Seems you met a trucker back in Hollis who was fit to be tied that you insisted on driving this way, so he put the call out on his radio, and every trucker what's spotted you between Hollis and here has reported your location to the highway patrol."

Making a sound like an exasperated Chihuahua, he added, "You don't realize how busy the roads are until every trucker on them starts calling in to dispatch. Then you've got somebody in New Mexico who called in a favor with one of our senators. Nearly every highway patrolman in this half of the state of Oklahoma has been tasked with locating y'all. I got the job of keeping an eye on Nowhere. I've been driving by here every hour for the past six."

Gavin gazed back at Avery who said, "Mitchell. He's got

interesting friends all over the place."

"So, anybody want to tell me what happened to the car?"

Eli jumped up, his phone slipping from his grasp and landing with a soft *kwang* against his abandoned seat. "The car rental company went to the wrong place and didn't pick us up. By the time they figured out the problem, they'd already given our rental SUV away to somebody else. They offered us a Zeon, but my mom here," he said, indicating Avery with the tilt of a thumb, "wouldn't hear of it."

The officer ogled them and their pile of luggage and said, "Uh-huh."

"So they stuck us with this little hatchback. It wouldn't have been so bad, but no sooner had we left Albuquerque, than we got food poisoning and a flat tire. When the tow truck fixed the flat, the back bumper fell off. That's when we realized the car was being held together by sturdy paperclips and a whole roll of duct tape."

"Uh-huh." The officer's eyebrows were climbing.

"The guy back in Moriarty is keeping the bumper for us."

"Moriarty?" The eyebrows lifted a bit further.

"Not too long after that, it started snowing. Then the radiator blew. Well, not really, but that's what we first thought. We called someone to come take a look at it, but we ended up with the guy who runs the bait shop because everyone else was gone. Only, he couldn't fix it. But at least we knew the radiator hadn't blown. So we had to keep the heater off and stop often to let the engine cool back down. The problem was, the snow was getting worse, and we couldn't turn the heater on. And it was the middle of the night."

Giving her son a soft elbow in his side, Avery whispered, "You are having way too much fun with this."

An unrepentant grin on his face, Eli said, "For the first time ever, I'm hoping my English teacher makes us write a *What I Did Over Christmas Break* paper when school starts back up. And that she makes us present it orally."

Avery tried to fight the grin and match the patrolman's somber expression, but it was hard. If Eli did have to give a report about his Christmas break, she would need to find an excuse to be in his class that day. With his flair for the dramatic, it would be a fantastic presentation.

"Maybe we should get you loaded up into my car, and you can tell me the rest of the story along the way." He didn't look as if really wanted to hear the rest of the tale. "By the way, my name's Sterling. Officer Sterling."

Gavin reached out a hand to shake and asked, "So do we call you Officer or Sterling?"

When the highway patrolman made no move to answer, Avery said, "Our stuff smells pretty bad. Are you sure you want it in your car?"

Officer Sterling frowned and said, "I'm pretty sure you smell just as bad as your luggage, but there's nothing I can do about that. We should be able to get most of the luggage into the trunk. The three of you will have to cram into the rear seat. Any luggage that don't fit in the trunk I might be able to put up front with me."

Avery, who again needed to use the facilities, smiled weakly as she took the toilet paper and headed out behind the little store. She heard Eli say, "Don't ask," as she slipped around the side of the building. With any luck, they'd have the luggage all loaded up before she returned.

**** 

"Sorry about the wind," Officer Sterling said to them as he pushed the button to lower both front windows. "I've got to do something to try to keep the stink out of my face, or I won't be able to see to get us back to Lawton. Man, oh man, it's been a long time since I smelled anything as fierce as this. It's a tenacious smell, too, ain't it? The folks in the garage are going to spend weeks trying to get the smell out of this car, and I ain't even the one who hit the little varmint."

"Uh, yeah, it's a strong smell alright," Avery said, not entirely sure if the officer even wanted a reply.

"It burns, too," Officer Sterling added. "Burns something fierce. I think my nose hairs might have been singed off. And my eyes feel all dry and crackly like firewood that's about to explode. Except for when the tears start pouring out, I guess. And don't even get me started on the nausea. How it is y'all aren't back there puking your guts out from having to smell yourselves is beyond me."

*How do you think it feels to be back here next to two other people who suffered the same malodorous fate? You've got it easy up there, mister!*

"Whoo-whee, that sure is one awful stench!"

"Okay," Gavin cut in. "We get it. The smell is dreadful, and it's not going away. What's supposed to happen to us when we get to Lawton?"

"Well," said Officer Sterling, "I suppose you can book a flight and head on back to Albuquerque."

"Peachy," Eli commented. "If you can't stand to have us in your car without the windows open, how are we supposed to fly back? The folks on the airplane won't be able to open their windows and blow the smell out of their faces."

"Hmm, you got a good point there," he answered. "Let me see what I can do."

Officer Sterling then proceeded to pick up his radio and call dispatch, "Hey there, Norma Sue, you read me?"

"That you, Joe?" came the disembodied high-pitched voice over the radio.

*Aha! So his first name isn't Officer after all!* A little giggle escaped, causing Avery's seat companions to look at her oddly.

"Yeah, it's me. I found those three travelers out at Nowhere, but we got us a problem."

"They look as scary as a bunch of serial killers? Maybe

cannibals? Should I call SWAT?"

Officer Sterling glanced over his shoulder at them and blushed. In a loud whisper he said, "Hush, Norma Sue. They're in the car with me."

The equally loud whisper came back over the speaker, "Oh, sorry about that. They're not threatening to eat you, are they?"

Avery, who was stuck in the middle between Eli and Gavin, could feel both men shaking with laughter. Even she had to admit the conversation was a short distance from absurd. "Who needs Vaudeville?" she asked in a whisper soft enough that her voice wouldn't travel beyond the back seat. The shaking beside her increased.

"So, uh, here's the deal," Officer Sterling said into the radio, now back up to his regular volume. "Their car's dead. I left it at Nowhere. They hit a skunk, though. The young'un's worried they won't be allowed on an airplane smelling as bad as they do."

"Whoo-whee," Norma Sue sang out in her whistling nasal voice. "That's the worst stink there is. And you got them in the car with you? All three o' them? Ain't no way the folks at the garage are gonna smile at you when you bring that car in. They'll stick you with that twenty year old clunker of a patrol car for at least the next month if you make them clean out skunk smell."

"Well, what did you expect me to do? Leave them out there to freeze to death?"

"Nah, you can't do that," Norma Sue answered. "Some big, high monkey-monk from the state has been breathing down Cap'n's neck." If the woman had paused even once to breathe, Avery couldn't tell. "Oh! I should let Cap'n know you've found them!"

"Wait!" Officer Sterling called, but it was too late. Norma Sue was gone.

"Wow," Eli said. "I didn't know they could put their own

officers on hold."

If the glare burning its way through the rearview mirror was any indication, Officer Sterling did not appreciate the observation.

Changing the subject, Gavin asked, "You have any idea why I haven't been able to get a signal for my phone? My cell service has been on the fritz almost this whole trip."

Officer Sterling let out a low whistle. "You know how college kids go home during Christmas break?"

When they all nodded, he continued. "Seems like a buncha kids at some college back east didn't have family to go visit, or couldn't afford it, or something. They stayed on campus over break and decided to prank a cell company by hacking it and doing something or other."

Avery winced, sure this tale wasn't going anywhere good.

"While they were in there poking around, they triggered some sort of worm that was in there from a long time ago. Seems like real bad security if you ask me." A brisk tap to the steering wheel emphasized his point. "Anyway, the news has been calling it a 'catastrophic failure'. People who have their phones through that company have mostly been without service since day before yesterday."

"Any idea when they'll have it back up and running?" Gavin ran a hand over his face as soon as he'd asked the question. He didn't appear too optimistic about the answer.

Officer Sterling shrugged. "They said forty-eight hours, but that was about two days ago. Not sure what they're saying now. My phone's through a different company, so I haven't been following. All I know is we increased patrols in the rural areas in case people got stranded and couldn't call for help."

Several minutes later, Norma Sue's voice came back over the radio, "You still there, Joe?"

The man in question expelled a heavy sigh before picking up the mouthpiece and replying, "Where else would I be?"

"Cap'n says you won't find an airline willing to sell 'em tickets if they're rank with skunk, plus the airlines are all backed up because of closures. He's got me calling around to hotels to see if I can find one willing to take them long enough so they can get cleaned up. I'll let you know what I find."

"A'right Norma Sue. I sure do appreciate the help."

After a couple moments of silence, Gavin asked, "So, is it true tomato juice is the way to get rid of skunk smell? I imagine it would stain the clothes."

Officer Sterling laughed. "My wife swears by tomato juice, but my mama, she has another solution. Mama used to take a whole bunch of hydrogen peroxide and mix in some baking soda and dish soap and make us wash down with that outside before we could come in whenever we ran into a skunk. Stuff worked like a charm," he said. Then, with a chuckle, "But don't you ever tell my wife I said so. She'd be madder'n a hornet if she ever thought my mama was better at something than she was."

"What about clothes?" Avery asked, thinking of all the bulging suitcases that were no doubt permeated with the same horrible smell.

"I don't rightly know, but I can call and ask Mama when we get back to the station. We want to make sure we don't mess it up. Wouldn't do no good to blow something up on accident, would it? Course that would probably get rid of the skunk smell just as well."

Avery laid her head against the back of the seat and closed her eyes. Her head was pounding from the smell and the constant droning of the wind through the windows. She thought about reaching for her purse to get some acetaminophen but rejected the idea. *What if the pills taste of skunk?*

Officer Sterling said, "You know, I've had people puke in my car before. I've had people bleedin' all over in the back seat. Had people urinate in the cruiser. Even had one man, you know, do the other, one time. But ain't none of that ever come close to smellin' as bad as the three o' you."

Apparently content to hear his own voice, he continued. "The thing about skunk is, the critter don't have to spray you direct in order for it to stink. When you hit it the way you did, the smell got air-o-saul-ized," he slowly enunciated the word. "That means the stink got up into the air. You walk through air reeking of skunk, and you come out the other side smelling almost as bad as if the little varmint had lifted its tail and sprayed you down personal-like."

There wasn't anything to be said to that, so Avery kept her eyes closed and prayed for the ride to be over soon. She needed something for her pounding head, and, if the officer insisted on continuing to talk about how bad they smelled, she was pretty sure she was going to need some antacids as well.

# Chapter Eighteen

Lawton, OK
December 25, 1:30 a.m.

They arrived in Lawton. Gavin, who peered at the darkened city around them, was not impressed. "Tell me again why we didn't go to Oklahoma City?"

Officer Sterling shrugged and said, "Nowhere is under the jurisdiction of Highway Patrol Troop G, and the headquarters are here in Lawton. S-O-P says I got to take you back to my station."

"What's the population of this place, anyway?" Eli asked as he, too, scanned their surroundings through the window of the police cruiser.

"Lawton here is the fifth largest city in the entire state of Oklahoma. It's one of our – what do you call it? – metropolises."

"How many people live in this metropolis?"

Even from their seat behind him, Gavin could see the man's chest puff up with pride before he answered, "Almost one hundred thousand people here in Lawton. It's a fine city."

Gavin felt Avery's elbow in his ribs seconds before her words penetrated. "Albuquerque's not exactly New York City, either. All we care about is whether or not they have an airport."

Officer Sterling pulled up in front of a long white building, low-slung with multiple flat roofs that had a layered appearance. While not nearly as complex, it had the look of a Pueblo-styled structure, but it was white, with the drab look of an industrial building. When he pulled the car into a parking spot rather than around to the back of the building, Gavin couldn't help but ask, "Don't you need to take it to the garage?"

With the first full smile he'd given them since coming across them in Nowhere, Officer Sterling said, "They're all off-duty at present, it bein' Christmas and all. If they don't find the problem with the car until tomorrow or the next day, that's fine. And if I'm not here when they do discover it, all the better!"

He let them out of the cramped rear seat and began pulling their luggage out from the trunk and passenger seat. As they trudged toward the entrance, Gavin wondered about the type of welcome they'd receive. Joe had made it plenty clear he wasn't happy about them stinking up his car, and the smelly travelers had no reason to think the folks in the Highway Patrol headquarters would feel any different.

Before Gavin could voice his thoughts, a tiny woman came rushing out through the glass doors. "Oh, you poor things! You've had such an awful time of it! Who in tarnation would be traveling through a whiteout on Christmas Eve is beyond me, not that those Texans would even know what a whiteout is anyway. We didn't get more than a dusting of snow here. But that's all behind us now. You come in here and sit down, and we'll get you taken care of."

Her voice gave her away. "Thank you, Norma Sue," Gavin said to her.

The bottle-red hair, pulled up into what could only be described as a beehive on top of her head, bounced dangerously as she nodded and beamed at him.

"Our car got hit a while back, and I'm afraid Avery might have a concussion. Could we get someone to look at her?" Gavin continued.

Norma Sue ushered them into what appeared to be an interrogation room, complete with two-way mirror. "I'll put a call in to the paramedics. They won't mind coming on down and taking a look at all three of you." Scarcely stopping to breathe, she continued, "Y'all have a seat in here, and bring your luggage, too. I was told not to let y'in at all, what with the smell, but I can't see doin' that to a body on Christmas morning, can you? There's no airline that will take you, and I couldn't find a hotel either. The homeless shelter, who I thought couldn't turn anyone away, said no way, not unless you actually were homeless. Then they'd be obligated. Lyin' to 'em didn't seem right. So I called up Joe's mama…"

"You did? How's she doin'? I was gonna call her, too, about the skunk smell." Crestfallen, Joe glared at Norma Sue as though she'd cheated in a game and won the prize.

"Don't worry, you'll get your chance to talk to her. She run over to that big department store that's open all-night to buy everything we need and should be here any minute now."

"Well, if it ain't my big handsome law enforcing son," came a booming voice from the lobby. Gavin couldn't see the woman, but by the deep baritone sound of her voice, he almost expected her to have a full beard when she came into view.

"Mama! How you doin'? I was gonna call and ask about the skunk smell as soon as I got back here. Knew you'd be able to help." When Officer Sterling's mother came into view, Gavin had to cover his mouth to hide his laughter. Avery, who must have thought he was coughing, hit him on the back. Good thing she was too tired to put any *umph* into it.

Mrs. Sterling was easily six foot tall with the build of a linebacker, possibly even one with pads already on. Her platinum-blond hair was askew, and her lipstick was hot pink. *Nobody's hair can grow in that direction, can it?* As he was studying the hair, she reached up and adjusted it, putting it to rights again. *A wig! A platinum-blond wig. On a very... robust... woman.*

Bemused, Gavin watched the interplay between the three Oklahomans. Mrs. Sterling set down a dozen grocery bags on the table in the interrogation room. Then she pulled two pieces of paper out from — well, maybe they'd been tucked into her bra strap — and set them on the table. She pushed one toward Norma Sue and said, "Here's the recipe for cleaning the people up." Giving the other paper a shove toward her son, she added, "And this here's the one for the laundry. If you mix it up, I'll start doing their laundry for them. Norma Sue said I could use the jailhouse washroom."

Gavin, who had been trying diligently to follow the conversation despite his fatigue, asked, "What?"

Norma Sue came over and patted him on the back. "Don't you worry about a thing. Since we can't get no place to take you in, we're gonna see to you here. Cap'n said to do whatever I could as long as I didn't put nobody in danger. So we're gonna mix up this stuff here that you use to clean your bodies. It'll help get the skunk smell off real good. I'm gonna take the missus here to the ladies' shower in the jailhouse, and she'll be able to wash. When we're done, Joe here will take you and the young'un to the men's shower so you can both do the same. We've got nice clean prison jumpsuits for you to wear once you get showered, too, so you don't have to get into them nasty old clothes again."

"Meanwhile," Mrs. Sterling said, "I'll get to work in the laundry room. I'll be back in a jiffy to collect all the clothes in your luggage. Got me a foolproof recipe for gettin' the smell out. Never ruined any clothes, either," she said with evident pride. When Joe blushed and looked away, Gavin figured that his wife, with her own ideas about tomato juice, must have ruined something.

Gavin and Eli took a seat at the table in the interrogation room while Norma Sue led Avery away. Shortly after that, Mrs. Sterling wheeled in an industrial-sized, cloth-lined basket, the kind normally found in a laundromat.

"I don't want to go rummaging through your things. Ain't proper, you know. I'll let you load the clothes into the basket, and then I'll take it from there."

Eli and Gavin got to work emptying out the laundry from their luggage and putting it into the basket for her.

As they got the last of the clothes in place, Eli offered to help her push it down to the laundry room. Mrs. Sterling laughed and said, "No way they'd let you wander around these halls smelling as bad as you do, but it's okay, honey-child. I'm stronger than I look."

She exited the room, and Eli sat back down. Leaning toward Gavin, the boy said, "Does she think she looks weak? 'Cause I'm telling you, in a street fight, my bet's totally on her. And that's based on looks."

\*\*\*\*

A half-hour passed before Avery came back into the room to the applause of Officer Sterling and the *click-click-click* of Eli's camera phone.

"You don't smell nearly so bad now," Officer Sterling said as he greeted her with a smile.

"My mom in a prison jumpsuit. Someday these pictures will be priceless!" Eli's glee was tangible.

"Alright, gents. Your turn." The officer led Gavin and Eli away.

Avery had no more than sat down in a hard plastic chair inside the interrogation room when a commotion pulled

Norma Sue away from her side. A few seconds later, a paramedic stepped into the room and gave her a sympathetic smile. "Got skunked, huh?"

She nodded and added, "Before that happened, I took a fall and hit my head. I think I'm fine, but everyone thought I should get it checked out."

With a professional nod, the paramedic said, "My name's Greg. It shouldn't take too long to figure out whether or not you're having any troubles."

As Greg shined a light in her eyes, he began to ask her a series of questions. "Can you tell me your full name? ... When were you born? ... How did you get injured? ... Where are you now?"

Avery answered all his questions, and he said, "That's a good sign. You didn't have to stop and think about anything. Is the accident with the car clear in your memory, or is it fuzzy?"

"Clear. I remember it vividly. I almost wish it were fuzzy. I didn't know exactly where my son was when it happened. Not knowing if he was in danger was scarier than any of the rest of it."

Greg moved his hands over her skull. "Don't mind me. I'm just checking to make sure nothing's broken." When he found the lump he asked, "On a scale of one to ten, how bad is your headache?"

"Probably a four or five," she answered. "It's been a long trip, though, and I haven't had much sleep. I had a headache before I fell, too, so that might be making it worse."

"Any sensitivity to light?" His fingers felt for her pulse.

"Yes, but I think that's because of the headache. I normally get a little sensitive to light when I have a headache."

"Are you tired?"

She nodded. "But like I said, I've only had a couple hours of sleep in the last two days. I was tired before I hit my head."

Greg gave her a smile as he wrapped a blood pressure

cuff around her arm. "It's not an inquisition. I have to ask the questions."

Avery took a deep breath and tried to relax. She didn't want to end up in a hospital on Christmas Day. Finding a way home and crawling into her own bed sounded so much better.

After Greg removed the blood pressure cuff, he said, "All through. You have some of the symptoms of a concussion, but I think that's more coincidence than anything else. Do me a favor, though, and don't go crawl off in a corner somewhere to get some sleep. If you decide you want to be alone, make sure someone knows where you are. And if you have any sudden changes in balance, head pain, nausea, or your ability to think and answer questions, please take yourself to an ER immediately."

"Of course."

Greg quickly filled out some paperwork and held out a clipboard to Avery. "I just need you to read this and sign at the bottom."

Avery did as she was told then, exhausted from too many hours without sleep, lay her head down on the table in the interrogation room as soon as Greg left.

"Everything okay, sweetie?" Norma Sue asked as she stepped back into the room.

"Not too long ago we were traveling through a part of Albuquerque I don't often go to. We saw a homeless man pushing a shopping cart, and I wanted to reach out and cover my son's eyes so he wouldn't see," Avery said. "It was almost like I thought he should be protected from knowing how ugly life can be sometimes. I felt disgusted, too. I didn't mean to react that way, and I wasn't proud of it, but that's how I felt inside when I saw that man with his shopping cart. Now here I am in a prison jumpsuit, and there isn't a homeless shelter around that will even take me in."

"People down on their luck and people livin' high-off-the-hog got more in common than most folk realize," Norma

Sue said. "Some of them work hard, and some of them never lifted a finger a day in their lives. You can't be judgin' a person by their clothes," the woman said as she reached out and pinched a bit of the bright orange fabric of Avery's sleeve. "If you want to know what's goin' on in someone's life, you need to take the time to get to know the person."

When Avery lifted her eyes to gaze at the small woman, her attention was snagged by something in the older woman's eyes. *I guess it's taken me this long to get past that awful hairdo enough to notice the rest of her. Good thing she hadn't thought to judge me based on smell when we first met.*

"Do you normally work the holidays?" *Might as well start working on that getting-to-know-people thing now.* "Seems as if you'd have enough seniority to get out of it," Avery said to her.

Norma Sue shrugged as her eyes shifted away from Avery to stare at the wall. "I don't have anyone to spend the day with, so I don't mind. I'm semi-retired, but I try to take the holidays so the younger folk can be with their families. Someone has to work. Might as well be me."

"No kids?" Avery asked. That's when she saw it again. A twinge deep in Norma Sue's eyes. *I hit a nerve with that one.*

Norma Sue smiled, but it didn't reach her eyes. "I had two babies. Twins. One died within the first week, and the other died from crib death when she was four months old."

*So much grief in such a short time.* Avery's heart dropped into her stomach, as heavy as a cold stone. *What do I say?*

"My girls would be about your age now if they were still livin'. I'd be a grandma to some ornery teenagers, I'm sure. My girls would've been beautiful inside and out. Every man in the county would have wanted to wed them and raise a family."

Avery was still trying to find the right words to say when Norma Sue reached out, kindness in her eyes, and patted her hand. "It's okay. You don't have to say anything. Appreciate what you have each day you get to hug your boy there, 'cause you never know when those days will be over."

From deep within the recesses of the building, a phone rang. Norma Sue reached up to touch a button near her ear. "Oklahoma Highway Patrol in Lawton. How can I help you?"

Avery's jaw dropped. The kitschy Norma Sue she'd heard talking up to this point was gone. The woman answering the phone and speaking to a distraught person on the other end was all business, her voice soothing and calm as she hurried back toward the front desk to take down information and dispatch an officer.

A few minutes later, she came back into the interrogation room. "Sorry about that. Most calls get routed through 9-1-1 these days, but every now and then someone calls us directly with an emergency."

"That's okay. How long have you been doing this job?" Avery asked.

Norma Sue's shoulders dropped the tiniest bit. Her smile spread wide. It was the kind of smile you give when you're trying to cheer someone up, but Avery had a feeling the older woman was trying to cheer herself up. "I've been at this job nearly thirty years now."

Avery couldn't stop herself from asking, "What made you want to work with the highway patrol?"

Norma Sue patted her hair into place as though a few stray strands might make the almost-neon-red up-do too garish. Then she took a breath and said, "I sometimes beat around the bush, but I'll tell it to you straight, okay, sweetie? Seems to me you can handle it. Not many folks can, so I do them and me both a favor by keeping things to myself."

Leaning forward, Avery wanted to catch every word. She didn't fully understand what Norma Sue had meant, but she knew she was being given a special privilege.

"After my babies died, my husband had a real hard time. He wanted a big family, you see, but I had complications birthin' my girls, and the doctor told me I couldn't never have kids again. When they both died, my husband decided he wanted a different life than just bein' married to me for the rest of his years, so he took off. I never got around to finding myself another man."

A sad look on her face, the older woman said, "I was confused for a lot o' years and thought maybe no man worth his salt would want me since I couldn't have babies. It was a kind of dark time in my life. Then a friend told me I ought to start doin' for others and that I'd feel better if I did. So I started working for the OHP, and it turned me around. Suddenly people needed me, and things I did mattered. My friend hit the nail right smack on the head. Helpin' others makes a world o' difference."

"You never remarried," Avery said softly.

This time Norma Sue's smile traveled all the way up to her eyes, making them sparkle like a lake at sunrise. "Once I got over feelin' sorry for myself, I got comfortable with who I was again. I found out I didn't need a man to be happy. I was content to do whatever the good Lord asked, and I learned to let that be enough. Every day that goes by, I miss my girls, but I know I'll see them again someday, and when I do, I'll get to shower on them all the love I didn't get to pour out on them while they were growin' up."

Avery reached across the table to touch Norma Sue's hand. "Thank you for sharing your story with me."

"Pshaw," Norma Sue said. "It ain't nothin'. We all got a sob story somewhere in our background. Take Joe's mama, for instance. She's got a doozy of a tale that goes back decades, but you wouldn't know to look at her. I first met Laura Jean back in grade school. Even when we were six years old she was twice my size. She took up for me when other kids would pick on me on account o' how small I was. We been friends ever since. Laura Jean's the one who told me to get over myself and start doin' good for those around me. That woman's as strong on the inside as she looks on the outside, let me tell you. Here lately she's had a rough time of it. You aren't exactly seeing her at her best, but she's still a better person than most everyone else I know."

Avery, who thought Mrs. Sterling looked strong enough to step into the ring with the heavyweight champ of the world, couldn't help but wonder about what the woman had been through recently. She was trying to think of a polite way to dig into the story when the woman in question came marching into the room.

"Is anybody comin' to help me fold laundry? It's not perfect, but the smell's a lot more tolerable now." Looking at Avery, she added, "I'll send you home with the recipe so you can wash the clothes in it some more if you think you need to. After they're packed up tight in suitcases for a while, they might need another soakin'."

Smiling her gratitude, Avery said, "I'd love to help fold. I've been sitting in an ugly cramped car for way too many hours these past few days."

"I need to stay up here where I can keep an eye on the entrance, but you two go on ahead," Norma Sue said. "I'll send the boys down when they get back."

Avery followed Laura Jean, noticing for the first time since arriving, that there were a couple other officers in the building. "Where'd they come from?"

Joe's mother gave an exaggerated shake of her head, causing her wig to skitter a bit, and said, "I'm sure when the word *skunk* came over the radio, this place cleared out in a hurry. Now that y'all are getting cleaned up, it's safe for them to come back."

# Chapter Nineteen

Lawton, OK
December 25, 6:05 a.m.

The clock crawled its way past six in the morning, the sky starting to lighten with the barest hint of pink and gold at the horizon. Weary, the three travelers sat at the table in the interrogation room. Their laundry was all clean, but Norma Sue still hadn't been able to find a place willing to take them in. Mrs. Sterling had given Avery a list of everything she'd need to buy back in Albuquerque to make more of her special de-skunker if they ever needed it. Then she went on home to feed the chickens and get ready for Christmas Day.

Officer Sterling was due off-shift at six, but he was sticking around in case Norma Sue found a place for them and they needed a ride. "I might as well see things through and get y'all to where you need to be before I go home and wake my wife."

Avery, always the curious one, asked, "So what's the deal with your wife and mom. They don't seem to get along too well."

Crimson stained the officer's neck and cheeks faster than wildfire spreads in a high wind. "It ain't as bad as all that. Lauren's a city girl is all. Never lived on a farm or out in the country. Mama didn't have an indoor latrine till about a decade ago. The two don't quite speak the same language." Then, lifting his eyebrows, he said, "I don't know where she got the idea, but Lauren thinks Mama's intimidatin'. Says if it came down to a brawl between Mama and Paul Bunyan, she'd put her money on Mama."

Avery couldn't help the snort that escaped.

Gavin, who'd looked as if he was dozing, said, "If they both love you, they'll find a way around their differences."

Norma Sue came running into the room. "Joe, you got t' load their things now! Herm's waiting over at the airfield. He's gonna fly 'em back home."

Eyes widening, Gavin sat up and asked, "You found us a flight?"

Norma Sue nodded, hair bobbing vigorously. "Herm's an old friend. Went to school with me and Laura Jean. His son lives in Tucson. He flies out there for Christmas, but because of the weather, he's been grounded. Got the all-clear a few minutes ago. I caught him as he was heading out the door to the airport."

"Let us change out of the prison suits, and we'll be ready to go."

"There's no time!" Norma Sue said urgently. "He's on his way to the airport now. I promised I'd rush y'all straight out the door."

Joe, who'd jumped up as soon as he'd heard the news, was already out the front door of the precinct, hauling most of their belongings with him.

"Can we get through airport security in these jumpsuits?" Eli asked.

"It won't matter none if you don't get to the airport in time, now will it? I'm sure Herm's got a place you can change." Norma Sue shooed them with her hands. "Now get out of here and go home!"

Caught up in the smaller woman's enthusiasm, they all rushed out the front door, hauling the camera cases Officer Sterling had left behind.

Avery made it halfway to the squad car when she wheeled around and ran back. She grabbed Norma Sue up in a tight hug and told her, "Thank you for being such a kind person, for welcoming us, taking care of us, and finding us a way home. Have a blessed Christmas."

Norma Sue's face grew almost as red as her hair. *Maybe I hugged her a little too tight.* The older woman reached up and wiped a tear away from the corner of her eye and said, "Ah, sweetie, it ain't nothin'. It does my heart good to be able to do for others. You have a blessed day, too."

\*\*\*\*

Officer Sterling flipped his siren on in the quiet of Christmas morning. They didn't pass another vehicle all the way to the small regional airport, but the siren continued to sing out its discordant tune while the squad car lights lit up the still-heavy sky. Norma Sue called ahead to the airport and let them know Joe was coming with important passengers for Herm so airport security wouldn't panic when he came blazing through.

Panic, as it happened, was the last thing on anyone's mind. A good two dozen people stood around Herm's airplane as Officer Sterling pulled his car into the hangar. The curiosity on people's faces moved from mild to rabid in a hurry when they noticed three people in prison jumpsuits getting out the back of the squad car.

A grizzled old man moved away from the plane and inspected them closely in all their bright orange, prison-jumper glory. Turning to Officer Sterling, he said, "Norma Sue didn't say anything about them bein' prisoners. Do I have to worry about them slittin' my throat while I'm in the air?"

Avery thought a funny comeback appropriate. Officer Sterling, however, was going to have none of that. He was as solemn as could be when he said, "No, sir. No need to worry about that. I don't think none of them can fly, so they'll need to keep you alive while you're in the air."

Before she knew what was happening, Avery was belted into a seat next to Herm in the cockpit, while Eli and Gavin were in the two seats behind them. The luggage was stored, and they were taxying for takeoff.

As soon as they were in the sky and Herm's attention wasn't required to talk to the sleepy folks at the tower, Avery told him, "We're actually nice people. There was a bit of a mishap with a skunk, and that's why we're dressed in these jumpsuits. I wanted to change before we left the police station, but Norma Sue said we had to hurry."

Herm chortled and said, "Norma Sue told me all about it. I can't help but give young Joe a hard time. He's such a serious fella. Been that way his whole life."

After a couple minutes, Herm asked, "So how is Norma Sue doin', anyway? I haven't seen her in a while."

Avery answered, "She's a spitfire and nice as can be. Christmas is hard for her, I think. I hope she has friends to spend the day with."

Keeping his gaze focused on the instruments in front of him, Herm asked, "You know if she's seein' anyone?"

She couldn't have stopped the grin that stretched her mouth wide if she'd wanted to. "We talked a little bit, and it sounds as if there's no one special in her life at the moment. Why? Are you interested?"

Herm shrugged, still avidly staring at his controls. "I've been thinkin' about it. Norma Sue and I go way back. Known her forever, it seems. She's a good one, through and through. Not a mean bone in her body. She was a vixen in her younger years, but she's aged well. Like a fine wine, I suppose. More mellow than she used to be, but still full-bodied and full of zest. You can tell by her hair, you know. But underneath all that, not a truer friend could be found."

Avery leaned back in her seat and asked, "You're going to see your son, right?"

Herm nodded.

"What about your wife?"

A gruff laugh escaped him before Herm said, "You're not a subtle one, are you?"

"I wouldn't know subtle if it jumped up and bit me on the backside."

His shoulders still shaking with laughter, Herm said, "My wife passed away some ten years ago now. Loved her like crazy. Took me a long time to get over it. I've been thinkin' lately is all. It don't seem right for a person to have to spend every day alone, and, I don't know – Norma Sue kind of came to mind." Herm tossed a quick glance her way before adding, "You probably think it's crazy, a guy as old as me thinking about courtin' someone."

Reaching her hand out to rest on his forearm, Avery said, "Having a chance at some God-given happiness and turning your nose up at it – that's crazy. Thinking Norma Sue is special enough to spend some time with – that's common sense."

\*\*\*\*

The remainder of the flight passed quickly. It was coming up on ten in the morning when Herm taxied his airplane up near the terminal at the Albuquerque Airport. He pulled the plane to a stop and twisted around to face his passengers. "There's no lavatory in here for you to change, but those jumpsuits aren't going to work at this airport. They don't know me here, and I'd rather not get bogged down with security, if you don't mind. I got a son and grandkids to go spend Christmas with. Dig through your luggage and find some baggy clothes you can pull on over those suits, and then we'll get you out of here."

Everyone did as they were instructed, and before long, Herm was opening the hatch of the airplane and allowing everyone to climb out. "You got anyone to pick you up?" he asked.

Gavin shook his head and said, "Nah. We were thinking we'd rent a car."

Eli, who had slept through most of the flight, must have thought that was the funniest thing ever. He laughed so hard he started coughing. Avery pounded him on the back. "Tell you what, Eli. If they have a Zeon this time, we'll find a way to make it work!"

Herm waved as he climbed back into his airplane and started taxiing back toward the runway. Gavin, Avery, and Eli stood there on the tarmac with their collection of luggage and camera cases around them.

"Well," Avery said, "I'd like to be able to say it's good to be home, so let's get to it."

They picked everything up and started moving toward the terminal.

All of a sudden, they heard sirens blaring. They quickly scanned their surroundings until they spotted a police vehicle approaching from their left. Instinctively, they all froze. The big black sports utility skidded to a stop not too far from them, and the passenger door flew open.

"Thank the good Lord! How dare you send me all those dire texts and then never follow up to say everything's okay! You could have been coyote chow out there somewhere!" Mitchell grabbed Avery in a hug, then pulled Eli in for a smothering embrace. When he got to Gavin he said, "I ought to deck you for not taking better care of my favorite journalist." Then he hugged the photographer as well.

"How did you know we were going to be here?" Gavin asked.

"Some woman named Norma Sue tracked me down. Said she had connections, that's how she got my home number. She told me you were flying in. I didn't even know you'd been found, let alone alive. I was up all night so worried I couldn't even review the upcoming editorials. Didn't it occur to you to call me when you'd made it to safety? No. Of course not. Let's all take care of ourselves and not worry one bit about poor old Mitchell back in Albuquerque, frantic with worry."

Avery put her arm around Mitchell's shoulders and said, "Sleeplessness seems to work for you. You're in fine form there, Mitchell." With a big sigh, she said, "It's good to see you."

Mitchell winked at her and said, "Load up, everyone. I pulled in a favor to get a ride to the airport so I'd have a vehicle big enough to haul all of you back home. My car can't hold much more than an empty backpack by the time you stick four people in it, and I didn't figure Gavin would want to put his cameras in airport storage."

After everyone belted in, Avery asked, "Are you going to tell us why we ended up on a trip to a town that barely exists?"

Mitchell snorted. "Some nitwit at Corporate made a list of places for you two to feature. He apparently picked them because the names had good media appeal and would play well in the paper."

"Nobody researched the towns?" Gavin's voice was incredulous.

Mitchell grumbled for a minute before answering. "They've now got some intern in charge of making sure the rest of your assignments are going to be worth the trouble."

Eli asked, "What happened to the guy who sent us to Nowhere?"

"Demoted to the mailroom would be my guess," Mitchell

answered with a shake of the head.

"When do we get to see the rest of the list?" Avery asked.

"I expect it in my inbox by Monday. I'll let you both review it then, and if you have any problems with it, I'll kick it back to Corporate. One thing is for certain," Mitchell said with finality. "There won't be any more wasted trips if I have anything to say about it."

"I wouldn't claim it was entirely wasted," Gavin said.

Avery felt the warmth of Gavin's gaze on her as he spoke. There wasn't anything she could do to stop the giddy schoolgirl grin fighting its way to the surface. For the first time in more years than she could count, she was completely okay with that.

**\*\*\*\***

Eli and Avery stepped over the threshold into their home. She closed the door behind them and leaned against it.

"That was the weirdest trip we've ever taken," her son said.

"Yep."

"And it's Christmas. It doesn't seem as though everything that went wrong could have happened in such a short time."

"Yep."

"You're not listening to anything I say, are you?"

"Yep."

Eli shook his head and started down the hallway. "I'm gonna take another shower and then crash in my room. You know where to find me whenever you want to open presents or get a bite to eat or something."

"Yep."

"But I might not wait for you. For food, anyway. I won't open gifts without you."

"Yep."

He'd already grabbed a fresh towel and was heading into the bathroom by the time he looked up to see his mom still leaning against the front door. Eli set his things in the bathroom and walked over to her. In an uncharacteristic show of affection that wasn't at all colored by the light-hearted humor they normally shared, he put his arms around her and said, "Merry Christmas, Mom."

As he pivoted back toward the bathroom, Avery swiped at a couple tears. She couldn't imagine how Norma Sue had survived the loss of two children, even if they had been babies and she'd gotten to know and hold them only a short time. *Maybe that makes it even harder.*

"Hey, Eli," she said. "I was thinking about maybe volunteering at the homeless shelter over by the rental lot sometime."

His eyes brightened. "That sounds cool. Could I come, too, or do you have to be eighteen?"

"I'm sure it'd be fine for you to come. I'll check, though, and let you know."

Eli bobbed his head in acknowledgment, a smile on his face, before ducking into the bathroom and closing the door.

Before she could change her mind, she sat down and booted up her laptop. A few clicks later, she found herself typing an email to the shelter's volunteer coordinator.

*I am writing to inquire about volunteer opportunities at the shelter. My son and I are interested in finding a way to contribute and help those whose situation or circumstances have put them in a place of need. Please let me know what opportunities would be available and suitable for a woman and her teenage son.*

After she clicked *send*, Avery surfed through some gift sites. She settled on a lavish gift basket of meats, cheeses, and sweet treats – all with a skunk theme – to send to Norma Sue and Laura Jean in care of the Lawton branch of the Oklahoma

Highway Patrol. *Skunk-themed gifts. Who would have ever thought?*

Then, before she could change her mind, she ordered a massive bouquet of winter flowers to be delivered to the station for Norma Sue. Avery read over what she'd written on the gift card five times before she clicked the *submit* button.

*You outshine all the stars in the sky and are more beautiful than any flower.*
*Regards,*
*Herm*

Between the two of them, Norma Sue and Herm would figure out she'd been the one to send the flowers. If the bouquet put a pitter-patter in the older woman's heart, though, then maybe it would help her agree to a date when Herm did come calling.

Once that was done, Avery plugged her phone in to charge and sent a quick text to Gavin.

*It was an adventure to remember. Next time Mitchell sends us on location, I say we demand hazard pay. Merry Christmas.*

A few minutes later her phone buzzed with a reply.

*Hazard pay, a luxury hotel with a hot tub, and a town that's actually there... that's all I'm asking for. Merry Christmas to you and Eli, too. Hope you have a great day and some good sleep, in any order you prefer.*

# Chapter Twenty

Albuquerque, NM
December 31, 8:00 p.m.

Gavin, driving his well-used sports utility vehicle, pulled up to Avery's house. This was going to be their first real date. He was looking forward to their time and hoped that ringing in the New Year together would bode well for things to come.

He climbed out of the car and began walking toward her front door. Partway up the path, he stopped and stared, confused. "Am I running late?" he asked Avery, who was sitting on her front stoop, a scowl on her face.

She looked weak-in-the-knees fantastic. Her brown hair was piled atop her head. She wore knee-high boots and a wine-red dress that somehow managed to flow loosely while still clinging in all the right places. Draped around her neck was a black silk scarf. He liked her penchant for scarves. One of these days he was going to have the freedom to reach out and tug on her scarf, drawing her in close for a kiss. They weren't there yet, but he hoped tonight would be the night that would start to change that.

Avery still hadn't answered him, so he approached and held out a hand to help her up. "Any particular reason you're sitting out here in the cold without a jacket?"

"My son locked me out of the house."

Gavin tried not to smile. "Why'd he go and do a thing like that?"

In her irritation, it didn't appear that Avery even noticed when he looped her arm through his and began leading her toward curb.

"I might have been having second thoughts."

*I'm going to have to buy something nice for that kid.*

"Second thoughts?" he asked casually.

Avery's free hand climbed distractedly toward her hair and fluttered for a second before falling back to her side. With a loud sigh, she said, "It's been eons since I've gone on a date. I'm kind of nervous."

Gavin opened the door with a sweeping bow and said, "Your chariot awaits, my lady."

Her eye-roll wasn't lost on him. Neither was the way her mouth tipped up at the corners or the touch of red that climbed up past her scarf.

Once he climbed behind the wheel and buckled his seat belt, he let out a chuckle. "This feels like familiar territory, doesn't it?"

This time she couldn't hide her chuckle. "There's nothing familiar about this roomy, sturdy vehicle."

Gavin turned to her and waited for her to make eye contact. The uncertainty in her gaze tugged at his heart. "You have nothing to be nervous about."

She looked away.

He waited. When her eyes returned to his, he told her, "You are drop-dead gorgeous and a great conversationalist to boot. And, to top it off, you've already seen me at my worst."

"I'm not sure that getting upset with the way our road trip went counts as 'worst'."

He winked at her, "I was talking about Rattlesnake Rest Area. Whimpering in pain and doubled over with cramps from food poisoning. Not exactly a stellar first impression."

Her smile widened. "To be fair, that wasn't the first impression you made."

Lifting an eyebrow, he asked, "Oh?"

She shook her head as he turned the key and listened to the ignition turn over. "Drinking some sort of hideous yellow concoction at a coffee house... that was the first impression I had of you."

Wincing, he pulled out onto the street, pleased to hear the strain leaving her voice. "Great. I'd happily forgotten about that."

At the first stoplight he came to, he turned and asked, "Did Mitchell tell you about his fight with Corporate?" When she shook her head, he told her, "He's trying to force them to buy a special kind of insurance policy to cover any disasters we run into when we're on an assignment they require us to take. It makes sense. Mitchell shouldn't have to foot the bill if he's not the one sending us on the trip. Corporate refused to take out the policy, but the last I heard, they finally said they're willing to amend the contract in regard to 'unforeseen disasters and the expenses therein incurred' – Mitchell's words, not mine."

"Good for him," Avery replied. "He needs to put his foot down. When the rental agency tried to bill him fifty thousand dollars for a replacement vehicle, he about hit the roof. He had no trouble telling them they were out of their minds. Corporate's not that different, I suppose."

"Mitchell's never been very good at allowing people to take advantage of him. He's the right man for the lead job at the Times."

Another couple of blocks passed by before anything else was said. "Thank you," came Avery's soft words from beside him.

Gavin glanced over at her and didn't want to pull his eyes away. She looked perfect, sitting there next to him. He'd already known she was beautiful, smart, and funny. Tonight was different, though. She was sitting in his car, a part of his life, and the emotional punch of it took his breath away. He finally managed to ask, "For what?"

"For asking me out, making me feel better about it, and maybe just a little for not laughing that it took my fifteen-year-old son locking me out of the house to get me to go on this date."

Gavin reached out and took her hand in his as he drove. He brushed his lips along the back of her hand and said, "Anytime."

# Epilogue

Holland, Michigan
December 25th (a year later)

"You have got to be kidding me!" Gavin's voice boomed through the hotel room.

Avery and Eli came running in through the door connecting the adjoining room.

"What's wrong?" Avery asked.

"No way!" Eli yelled.

"Shut it off!" shouted Avery.

"That's so cool!" from Eli.

Gavin reached out and hit the *clear* button on the microwave. "All I wanted was to heat up some of my leftover Hunan Chicken."

Giving him a puzzled look, Avery asked, "Did you put a fork in there with it?"

Holding up the plastic fork still in his hand, Gavin said, "No fork, and even if I did, it's not metal."

"I've heard of this," Eli said as he examined the charred remains in the bowl. "That was some light show, man. I've never seen a microwave explode before."

"It didn't explode," Gavin corrected.

"Try and tell the manager that when it's time to check out," Eli countered.

"What could make Hunan Chicken set a microwave on fire?" Avery wondered.

"Iron," Eli said.

"Huh?" Avery and Gavin both asked.

"Broccoli's high in iron. There have been documented cases where a microwave has responded to broccoli similar to how it would metal. Look here," he said, pointing to pieces of broccoli that were black and smoking. "If you look, you can see the broccoli's burned, but the chicken is still cold."

The smoke from the microwave reached the slow-witted and outdated smoke-detection system. Sputtering to life, the sprinklers in the room drowned them all in a sea of foamy mist. Gavin and Eli both dove for the bed where the camera cases sat, thankfully closed.

Avery, thinking to escape the shower, stepped over the threshold back into the other room. She enjoyed a few seconds of peace before the sprinklers in that room came on as well.

Picking up her purse, she strode out into the hallway and stood there waiting for Gavin and Eli to join her. The hotel's manager came running from the elevator. An alarm must have tripped downstairs to let the front desk know the sprinkler had been set off.

"The fire department's on the way! Is everyone okay?" he huffed in between puffs.

Avery gave him a weak smile. "No need to call the fire department. Apparently microwaves aren't always happy with broccoli."

Standing to his full height, all five foot three inches, the manager thrust his chest out in importance. "If a fire was started because of guest negligence, then the guest is responsible for any damages."

"Nobody did anything wrong. The microwave went wonky," Eli said.

"I can't cancel the fire department," the manager said, hands on his rounded hips. "The smoke alarm automatically alerts them when it's triggered, and hotel policy requires they come. If they arrive and there's no fire, they will issue a bill, and said bill will be passed on to the guest who led to a false alarm being sent in the first place."

Avery lifted her eyes to look at Gavin who stood there, two camera cases by his feet, and a black plastic take-out bowl of charred Hunan Chicken still in his hand. She lifted an eyebrow in question, and he gave a slight shake of the head. Then he mouthed the word *Mitchell* to her.

She nodded and took out her phone.

*Fire at hotel. Not really. Pretty much just smoke. Blame the broccoli. Manager says you have to pay for fire department being dispatched. Plus damages to room. Sprinkler probably destroyed televisions and beds. And at least one microwave has given up the ghost.*

After she sent the text to Mitchell she faced the manager and said, "You'll find the rooms were reserved by the Albuquerque Times. I've alerted our editor there to the dilemma. He can take care of everything for you." Putting on her best win-'em-over smile, she said, "Now, we need new rooms."

The manager shuffled his feet for a few moments before saying, "We're all booked up. There aren't any other rooms."

"Of course not," Gavin said, as he put down his chicken and picked up his camera cases. "I'll go load these in the car."

Eli had shown the wherewithal to run back into the rooms and rescue two suitcases. Extending the telescopic handles so he could pull them down the hallway, he said, "Right behind you."

Avery lightly patted the polycarbonate exterior of her suitcase as Eli ambled by with it. They had been an upgrade after a run-in with a hurricane during one of Corporate's edicts for a story in a small Texas town on the gulf of Mexico. Both hard-shelled and waterproof, the suitcases had proven their worth in the months since. As a bonus, buying hers in pink had guaranteed Eli would no longer snag it for his own packing.

"Well then," Avery said to the manager. "Can you think of any place in town that might have rooms available?"

Face now flushed, he avoided eye contact before saying, "The ice show is in town this week. Everything is booked up. Without a reservation, you won't find a room anywhere in town."

Avery picked up the bowl of chicken from the floor, placed it into the manager's hands and said, "This is what was in the microwave and caused all this fuss. I'm not sure who you want to take that up with, but the fire marshal might need to see it."

Then she picked up her purse and started walking away, a bounce in her step.

"Mrs. Eastly," he called after her, "there will be questions and paperwork. You can't just leave!"

More than halfway down the hall, Avery spun back to him and smiled, "I have a story to write and a deadline to meet. I can't wait around here. You have the contact information for the paper. The bill goes to them, anyway, and they signed as the responsible party. I'm sure you'll be hearing from my editor soon. Name's Mitchell. He's a bit of a bulldog, but he's used to things going wrong."

When Avery joined Eli and Gavin in the large yellow sports utility vehicle, she buckled in and said, "Every hotel in town is booked up. So where to?"

Gavin reached over and took her hand, bringing it to his lips and kissing the back of it. "Wherever you want, dear." Then he released her hand and shifted into gear.

"Gross," Eli said from the back seat. "You promised this

was going to be a working trip with none of that smoochy stuff."

Avery turned around to look at her son and said, "Can I help it if I'm enamored of my husband, Eli? We may have agreed to do a story while we're here, but that doesn't mean it's not still our honeymoon. In fact, since it is our honeymoon," she said, winking at Gavin, "I think we should stop to kiss every five minutes. It makes perfect sense, don't you think?"

"Absolutely," Gavin said. "I could go for every three minutes, but in deference to the moody teen in the next seat, I'm willing to settle for five."

Eli rolled his eyes, covered his ears and started singing at the top of his lungs. "La-la-la-la-la-la-la-la-la-la."

Avery blew him a kiss, and Eli stuck his tongue out at her.

"You know, Eli," Gavin said, "I'd have married your mom back in the spring if she'd have let me. I was ready to pop the question by the time February rolled around. She needed time, though, to come around to my way of thinking. So, really, you should thank her. If it had been up to me, you'd have been forced to endure all kinds of kissing for months now."

"Ugh," said Eli. "I hope I don't ever fall in love." Then he winked at his mom.

Eli had been her biggest cheerleader as she'd struggled with allowing herself to become emotionally involved with Gavin. Her son was the one who'd told her she'd never find anyone if she wasn't willing to risk her heart. So she'd risked it. What had followed was months of dating, laughing, travelling together to assignments – where something always went wrong – and feeling more fulfilled and alive than she'd imagined possible.

He loved Gavin, too, which made all the difference. Marriage to anyone would have been off the table unless Eli had been completely behind it. Mitchell had told her she was giving her son too much power over her and that she needed to put her foot down as the adult. She, however, had trusted her son, and it had paid off. Besides, it had been a fun year, and there wasn't much about it she would change. *Except maybe being forced out of our hotel on Christmas Day in the middle of small town Michigan.*

With a laugh, Avery reached out and took Gavin's hand. "Well, guys, since this is a business honeymoon, we might as well head toward Grand Rapids. I'll get on the phone and find us a room. We're going to need to stop in Wyoming on the way, though."

"Wyoming?" Gavin and Eli both asked, their voices as skeptical as their faces.

"Yep, Wyoming. It's a small town on the outskirts of Grand Rapids. At least according to the map. Exactly the sort of piece they enjoy at Corporate." Then, nodding enthusiastically, she said, "Maybe we can even find a room there." She held the map up and gazed at it, twisting it this way and that.

"You've got to invest in GPS, Mom."

"Ah, come on. What's the fun in that? Name once in the past year when having GPS helped us. Did it protect us from broken-down cars, spoiled food, bad hotels rooms, or blizzards? Did it keep us safe from power outages, tornadoes, hurricanes, or chocolate shortages?"

Her phone chirped to life, and Avery glanced down at it with an, "Ah, how sweet."

"What is it?" Gavin asked.

She showed him the picture on the screen. Norma Sue had sent her a picture of Laura Jean, her son Joe, and her daughter-in-law all huddled around a tiny little sleeping baby.

"Well, look at that," Gavin said. "Looks as if Laura and Joe's wife got over their differences."

"Norma Sue said as soon as Laura Jean's chemo finished

and she started feeling closer to her old self again, she and Joe's wife started getting along better. Having the promise of a grandbaby to dote on helped, too."

"When's the last time you talked to Norma Sue? How are she and Herm doing?"

Avery laughed. "Last time I talked to her, she was mad because Herm had suggested she try a different hairstyle. It seems her beehive is too tall for the cockpit of his plane, and her hair keeps getting smashed."

"Are they ever going to tie the knot?"

With a nod, Avery answered, "Don't dare tell Norma Sue this, but they've got a Valentine's Day wedding coming up. We're invited."

"She's getting married in less than two months and doesn't even know it?" Eli asked.

Avery shrugged. "Herm wants to surprise her. The whole town is getting in on it. There's not a person there that Norma Sue hasn't helped at one time or another. I can't wait to go."

"Oh no," Eli said. "We're going to have to drive, aren't we?"

Gavin laughed. "No rental this time. We'll take my truck."

Eli let loose with a hoop and a holler. When Gavin stole a look at him through the rearview mirror with a lifted eyebrow, the boy responded, "Rental agency insurance says I can't drive. Your insurance says I can."

With a pronounced wince, Gavin pulled the big, ugly, rental vehicle onto the highway and said, "Tell me which direction to go. Wyoming, Michigan, or bust!"

About to put his earbuds back into place, Eli said, "You know, I almost miss Nowhere. Almost."

Avery laughed as she eyed her son. "Nothing says adventure quite like the stink a skunk makes, you mean."

"Hey," Gavin said. "Don't knock the place. I met my new family on the road to Nowhere."

When Eli and Avery stared at him, he shrugged. "Too corny, huh?"

"Uh, yeah," came the reply from the back seat.

"A smidge," Avery said. "It's okay, though," she added. "We love you anyway." Then, for emphasis, she leaned over and gave her new husband a kiss on the cheek and said, "Right, Eli?"

"Sure, whatever," came the reply, "but I'm not kissing him."

# Acknowledgements

We all have those special friends who are beyond precious to us. I want to acknowledge some of those people who, despite knowing my faults, foibles, and idiosyncrasies, have still managed to love me.

An amazing person, a loyal friend, and an outspoken advocate – I lift my coffee mug in toast to Shari Schroeder, a woman whose belief in me has seen me through times when I haven't known how to believe in myself. She has allowed me to borrow her strength and common sense more times than I can count. *It takes a brave friend to say, "Stop making her spit out the water. It's getting old."*

An endless source of wise council, uplifting words, and lots of shared laughter – I salute Travis and Betty Best. It is an honor to know you both and a privilege to have you in my life. Thank you for loving my family in such a special way and for sharing your life stories with me, including the one about a young New Mexico police officer and a skunk...

Merry Christmas!

# About the Author

Aside from her long-standing love affair with coffee, Heather's greatest joys in life are her relationship with her Savior, her family, and writing. Years ago, she decided it would be better to laugh than yell. Heather carries that theme over into her writing where she strives to create characters that experience both the highs and lows of life and, through it all, find a way to love God, embrace each day, and laugh out loud right along with her.

Made in the USA
Lexington, KY
30 November 2014